THE BATTLE OF THE VEGETABLES

by Matthieu Sylvander

Illustrated by Perceval Barrier

Clarion Books

Houghton Mifflin Harcourt

Boston New York

For Mamie Jeannine
—Matthieu S.

For Françoise and Jacques Barrier
—Perceval B.

Clarion Books
215 Park Avenue South
New York, New York 10003

Copyright © 2013, *l'école des loisirs,* Paris

First published in France by *l'école des loisirs,* Paris.
First published in France by *l'école des loisirs* under the title *3 contes cruels.*
Published in English in the United States in 2016.

Clarion Books is an imprint of Houghton Mifflin Harcourt Publishing Company.

www.hmhco.com

The text was set in Agenda Light and Basha.
The illustrations in this book were done in india ink for drawing
and color ink for coloring.

Library of Congress Cataloging-in-Publication Data is available.
LCCN: 2014045632

Manufactured in China
SCP 10 9 8 7 6 5 4 3 2 1
4500558761

Cast of Characters

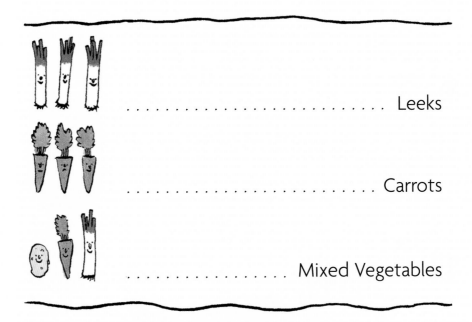

. . . . Leeks

. . . . Carrots

. . . . Mixed Vegetables

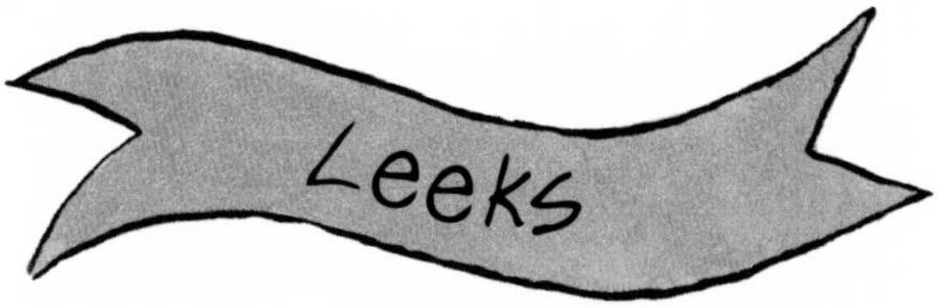
Leeks

Leeks are vegetables in the onion family.

In the vegetable garden, the leeks generally lead a calm, monotonous—maybe even boring—life.

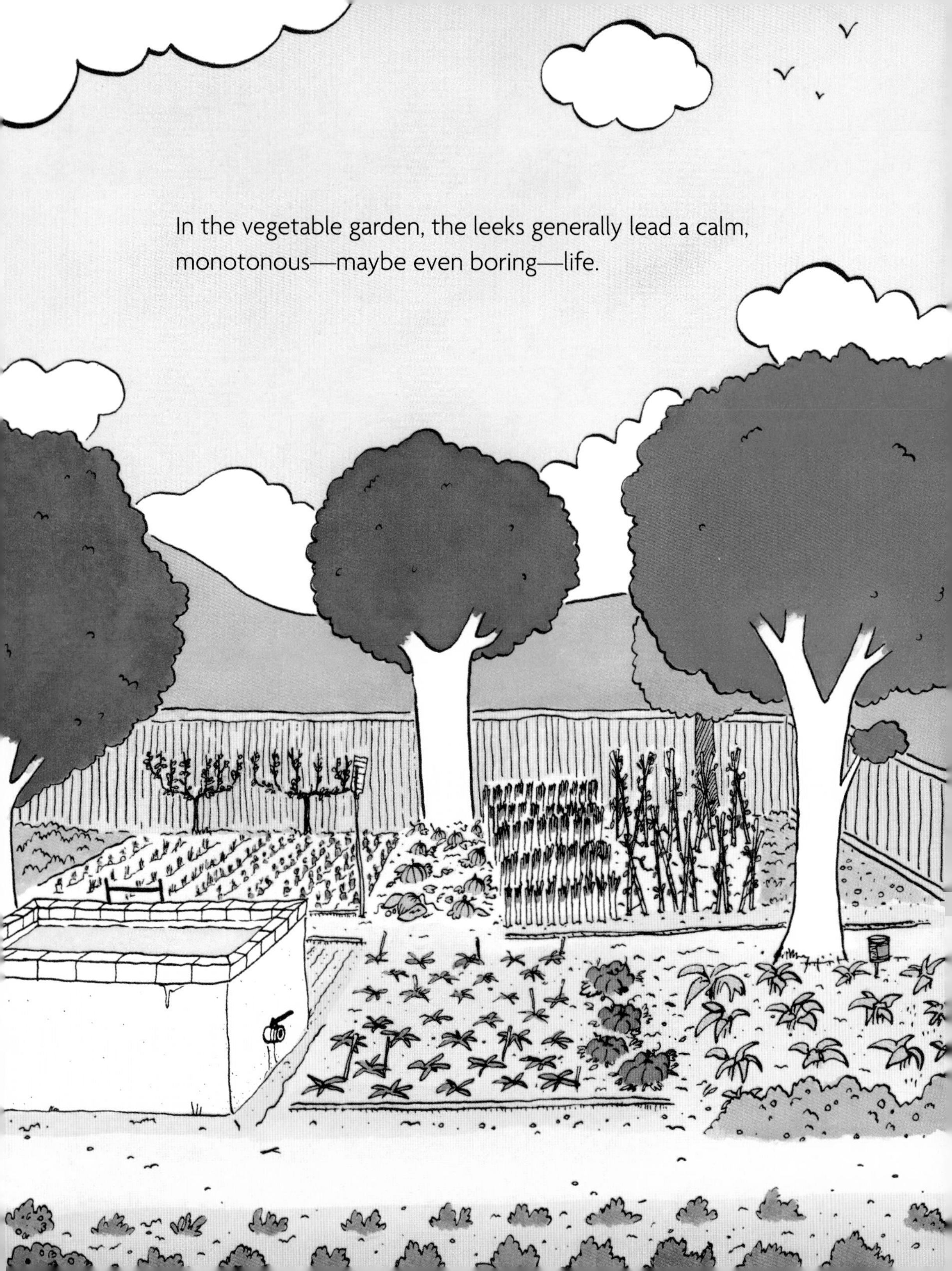

They have no distractions other than the wind. When the wind blows in the garden, the leeks feel as though they're running in the hills.

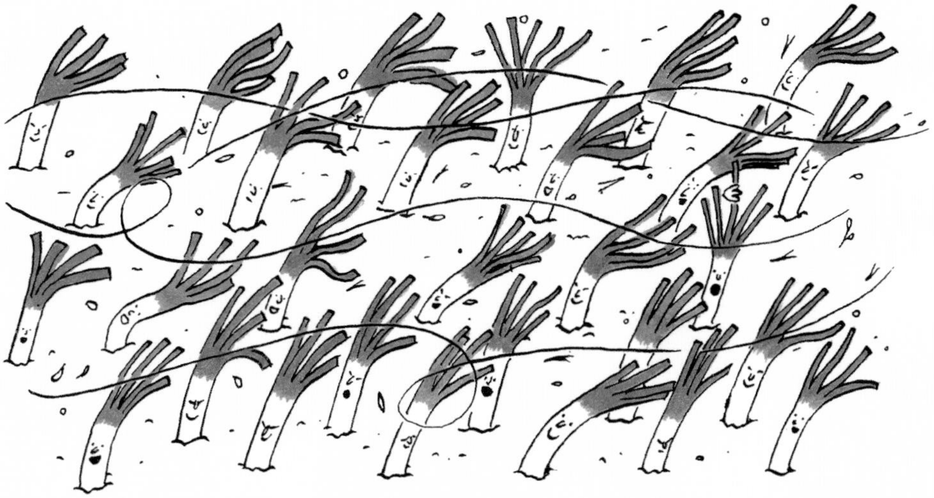

But leeks never run. They don't even have legs, only silly little beards.

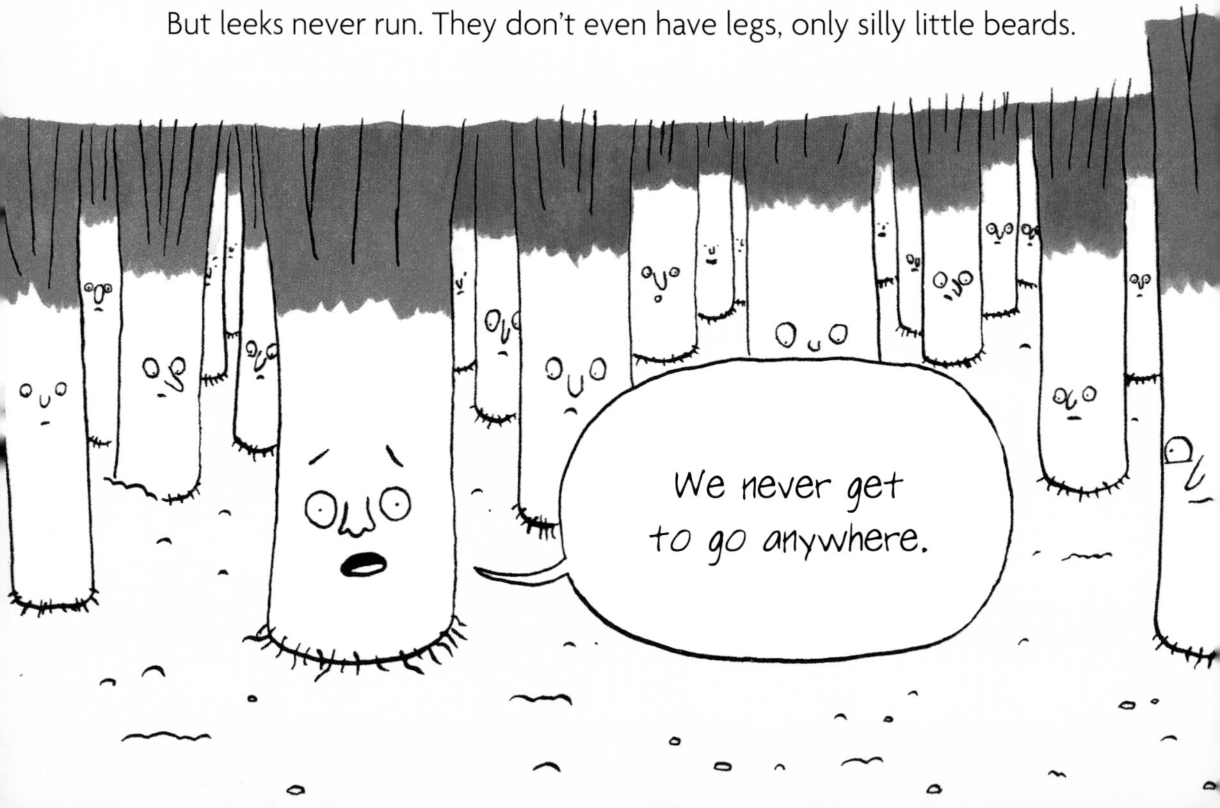
We never get to go anywhere.

That's why, when they think no one can hear them, the leeks love to talk about faraway destinations and exotic adventures.

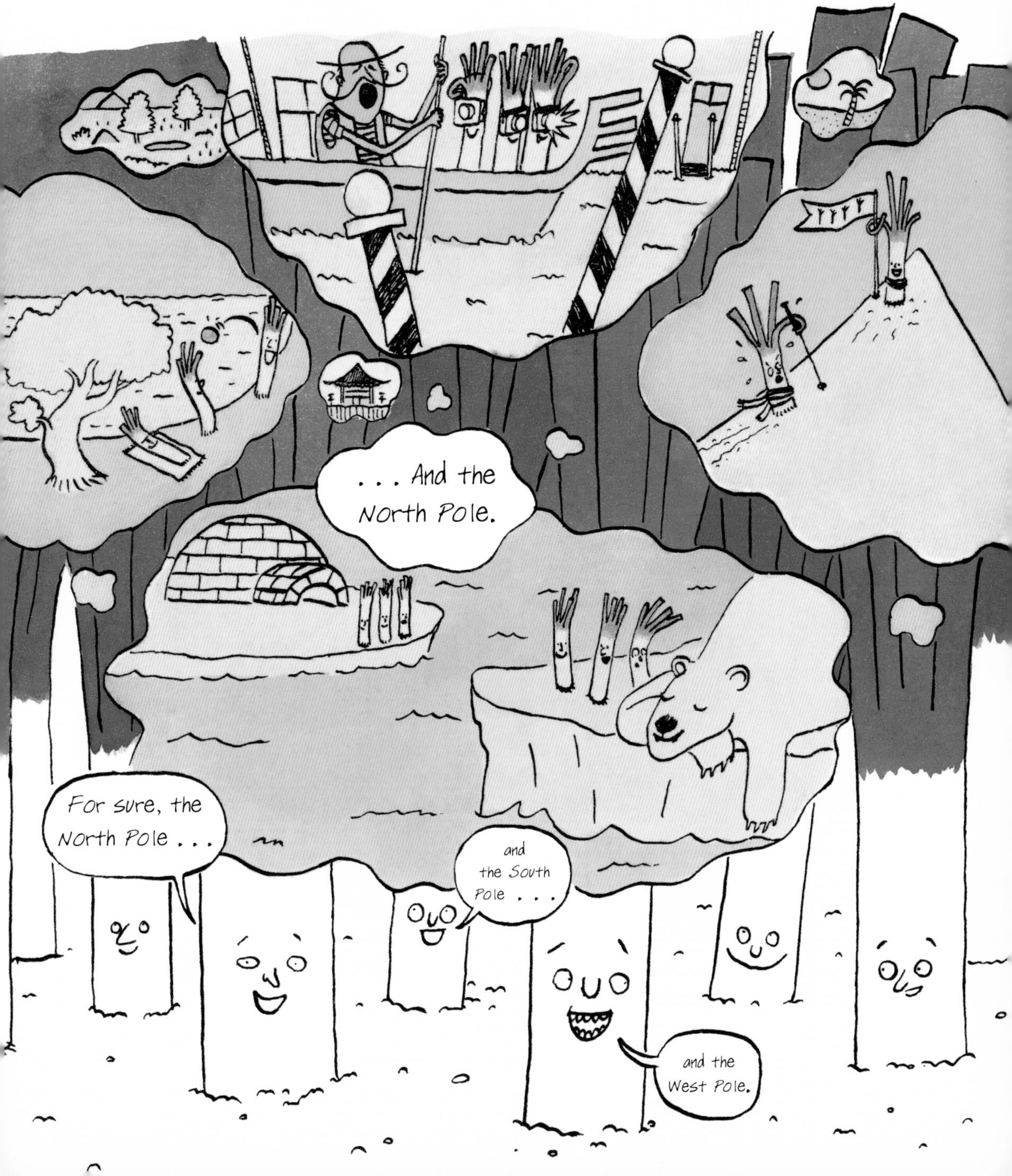

. . . And the North Pole.
For sure, the North Pole . . .
and the South Pole . . .
and the West Pole.

One day, when they're talking about igloos and seals, they suddenly see a big head looking over the fence. The leeks are a bit frightened. It's the biggest head they've ever seen.

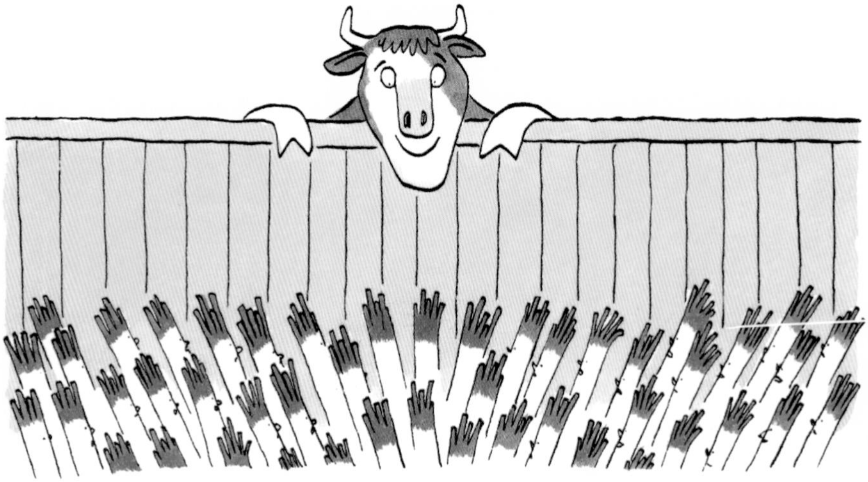

And the big head talks! It says in a very sweet voice:

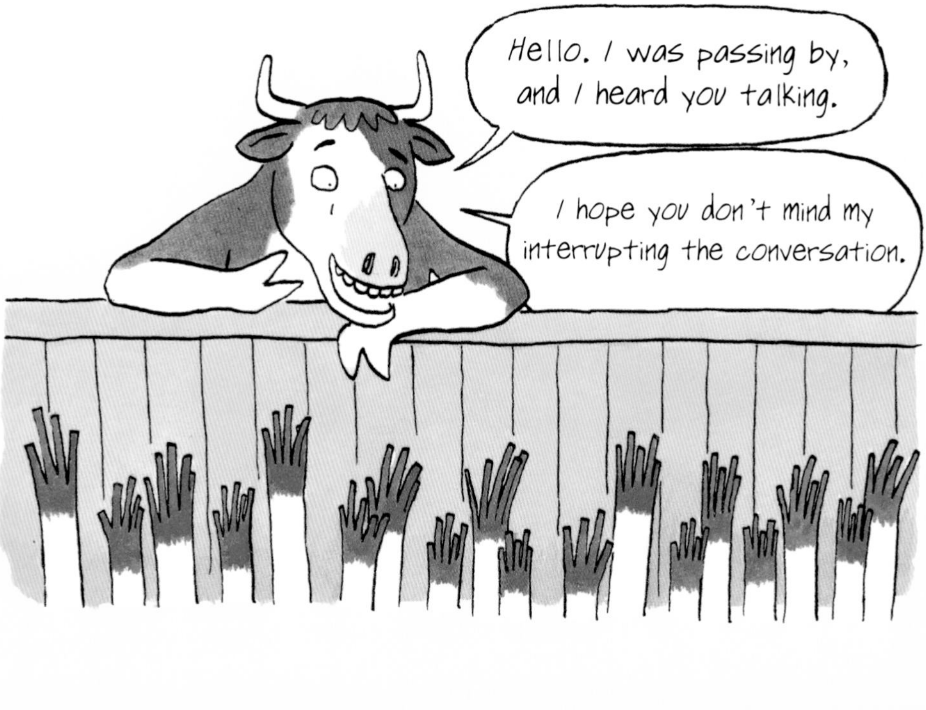
Hello. I was passing by, and I heard you talking.
I hope you don't mind my interrupting the conversation.

The leeks are thrilled! No stranger has ever taken an interest in them before.

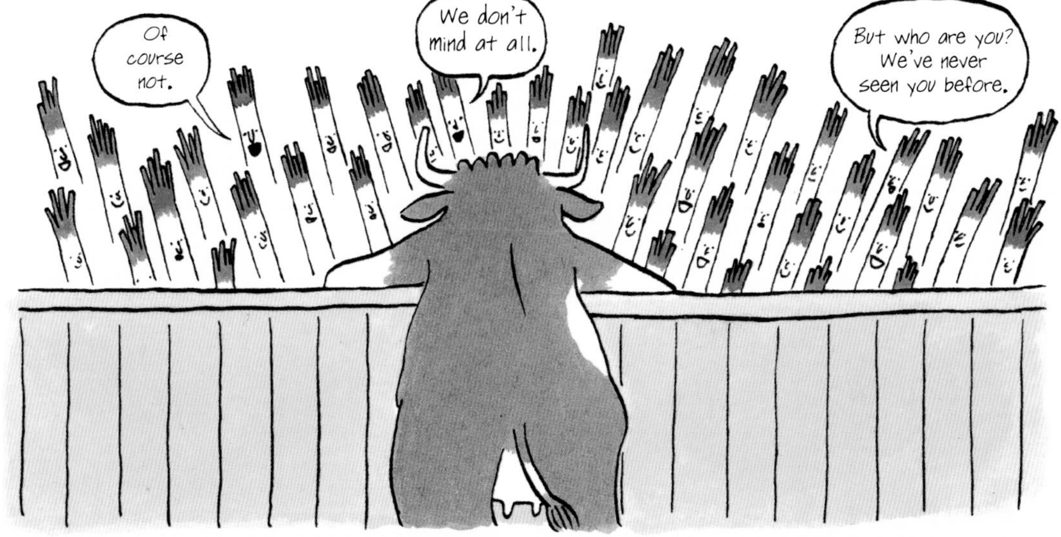
Of course not.
We don't mind at all.
But who are you? We've never seen you before.

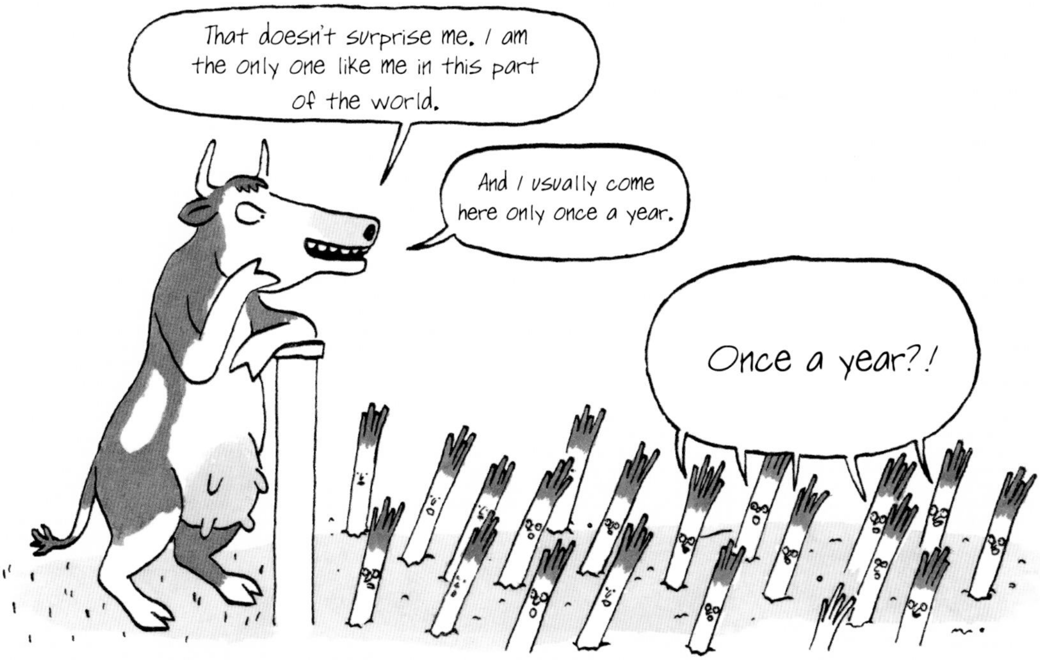
That doesn't surprise me. I am the only one like me in this part of the world.
And I usually come here only once a year.
Once a year?!

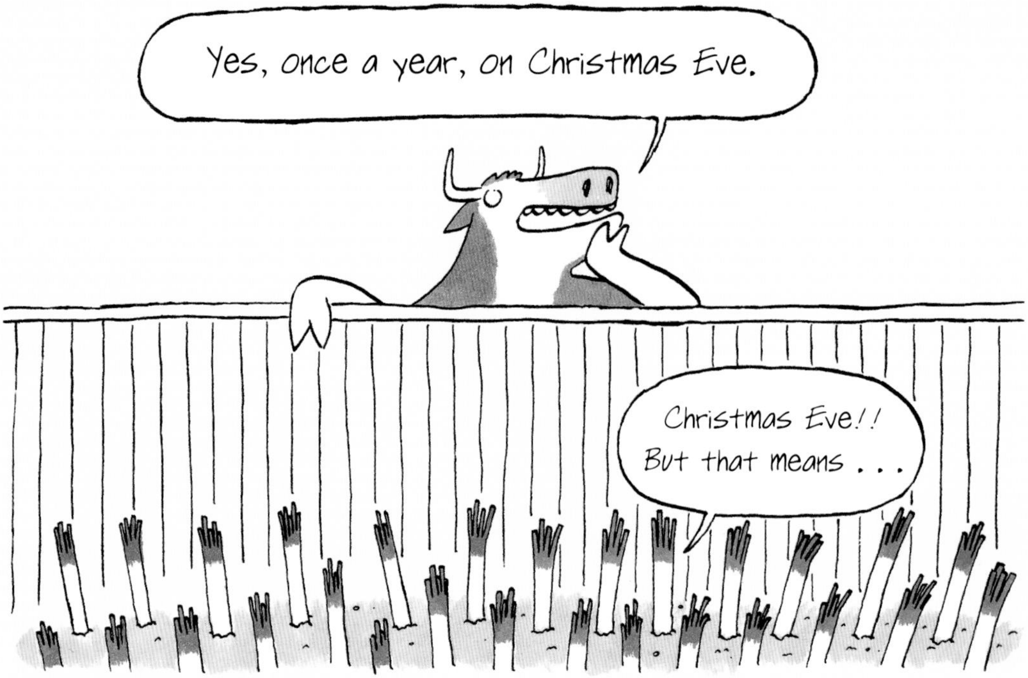
Yes, once a year, on Christmas Eve.
Christmas Eve!! But that means . . .

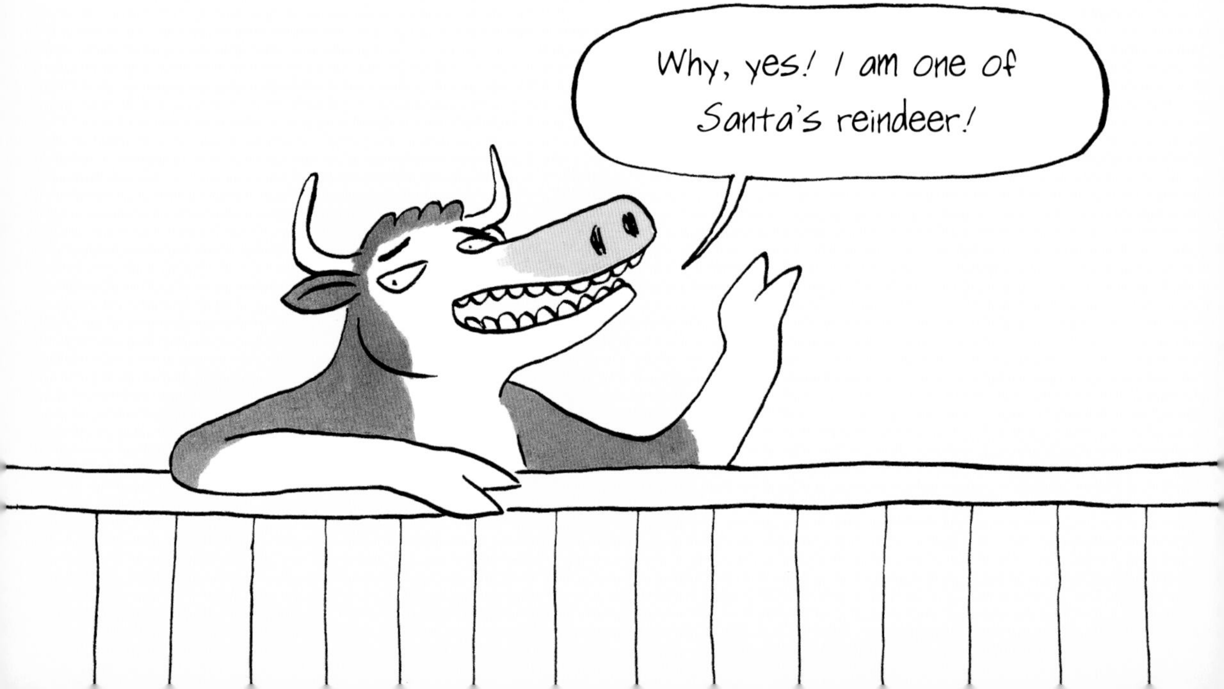
Why, yes! I am one of Santa's reindeer!

The leeks don't believe their ears. *Right there,* smiling at them over *their* fence, is one of *Santa's reindeer!* One of the most important personages in the *whole world!!* Three leeks faint, their delicate nerves overcome with emotion.

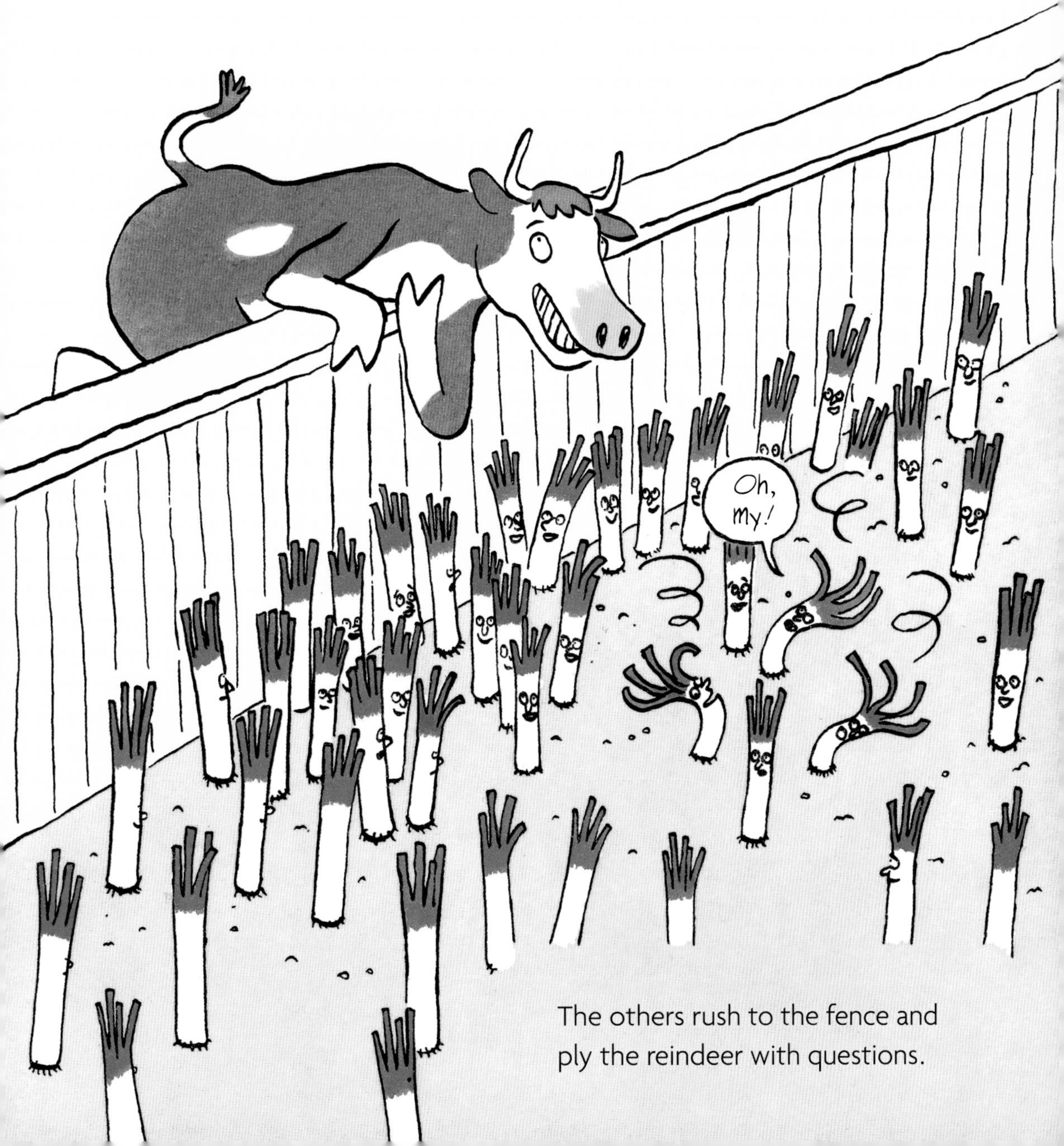
Oh, my!

The others rush to the fence and ply the reindeer with questions.

Yes, he's really the one who pulls the sleigh on Christmas Eve. He does it all by himself.

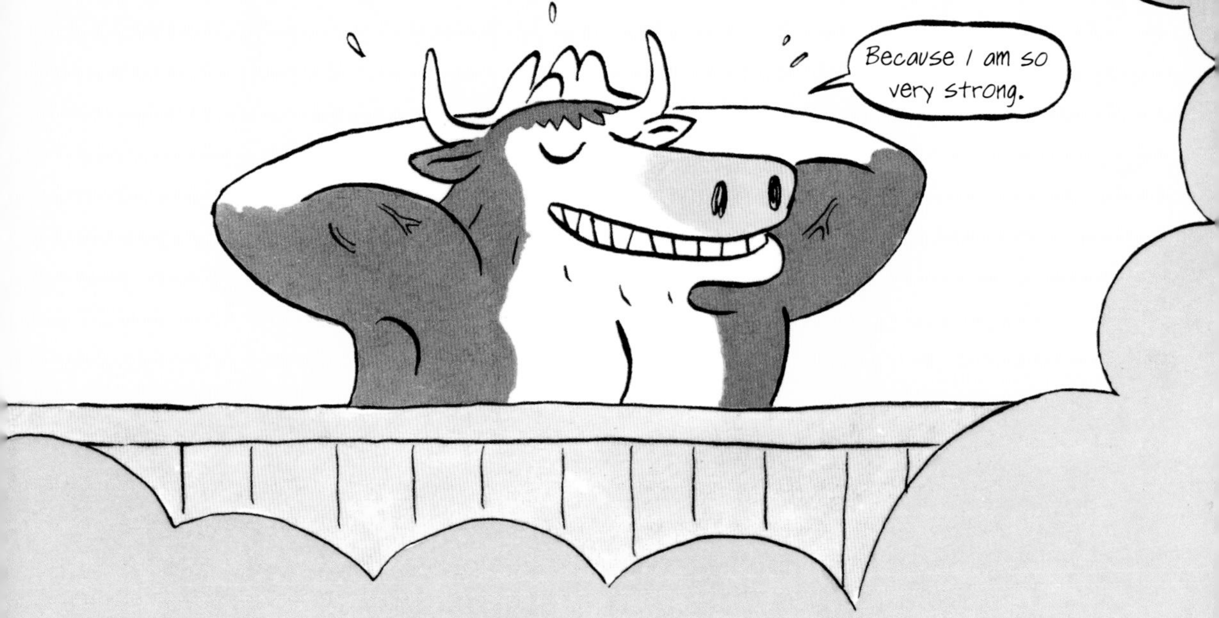
Because I am so very strong.

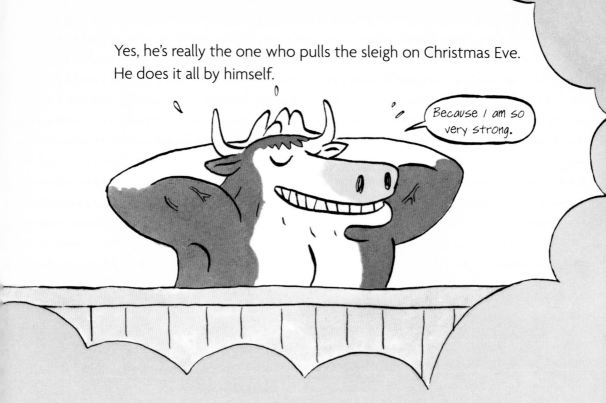

He lives in an igloo with a fireplace and curtains on the windows.

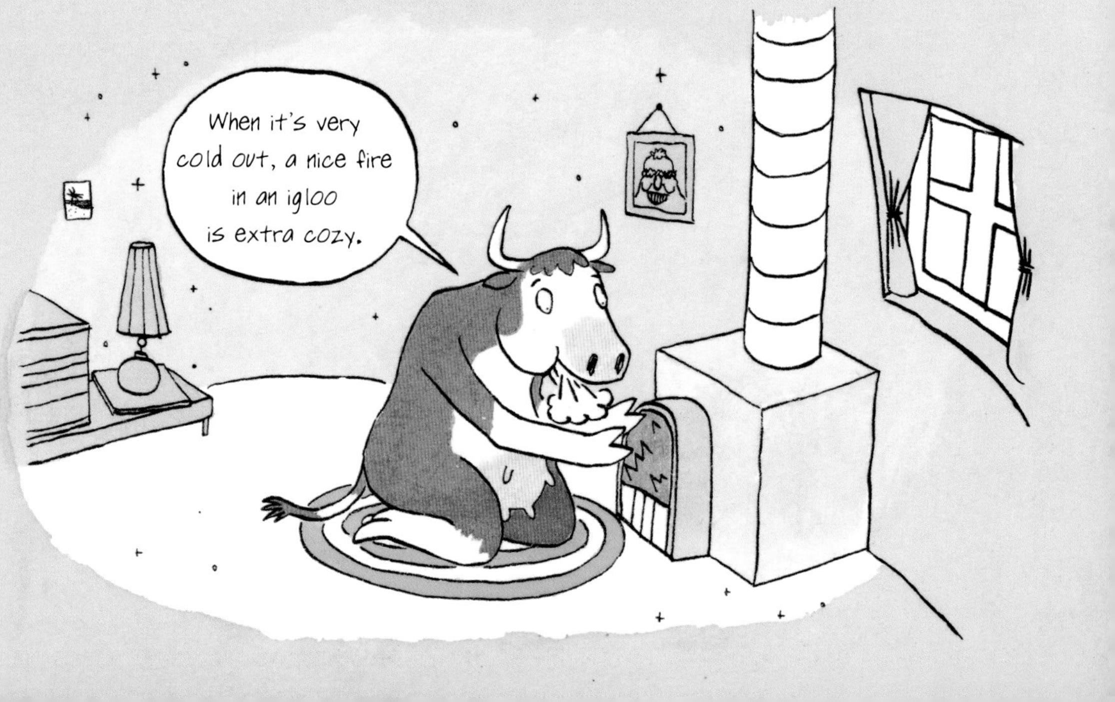
When it's very cold out, a nice fire in an igloo is extra cozy.

He eats *only* fish that he catches through a hole cut in the ice.

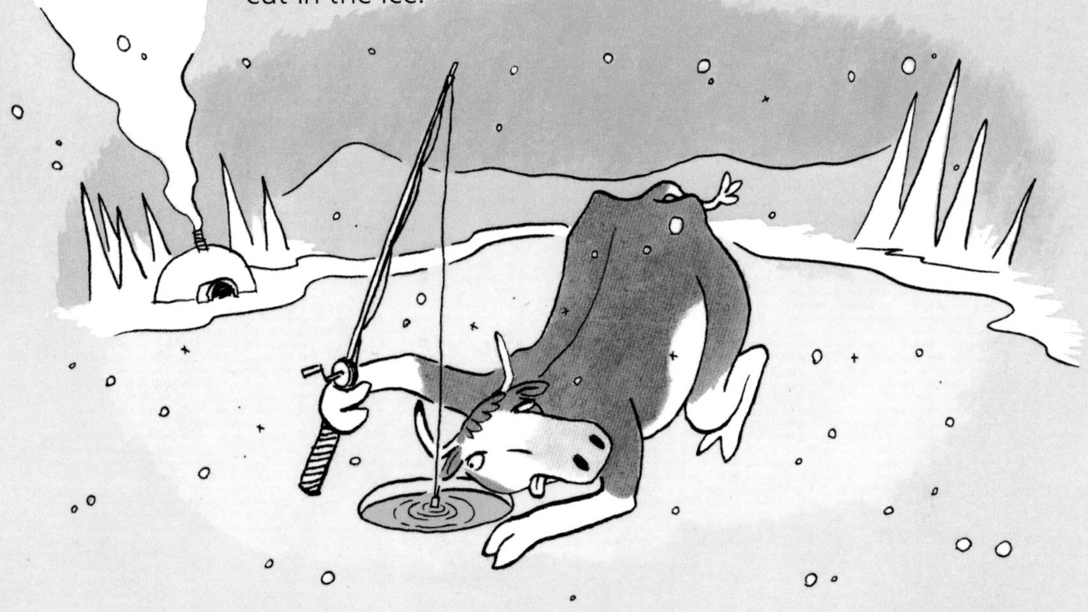

And he loves skiing on the ice floe. He's a superb skier.

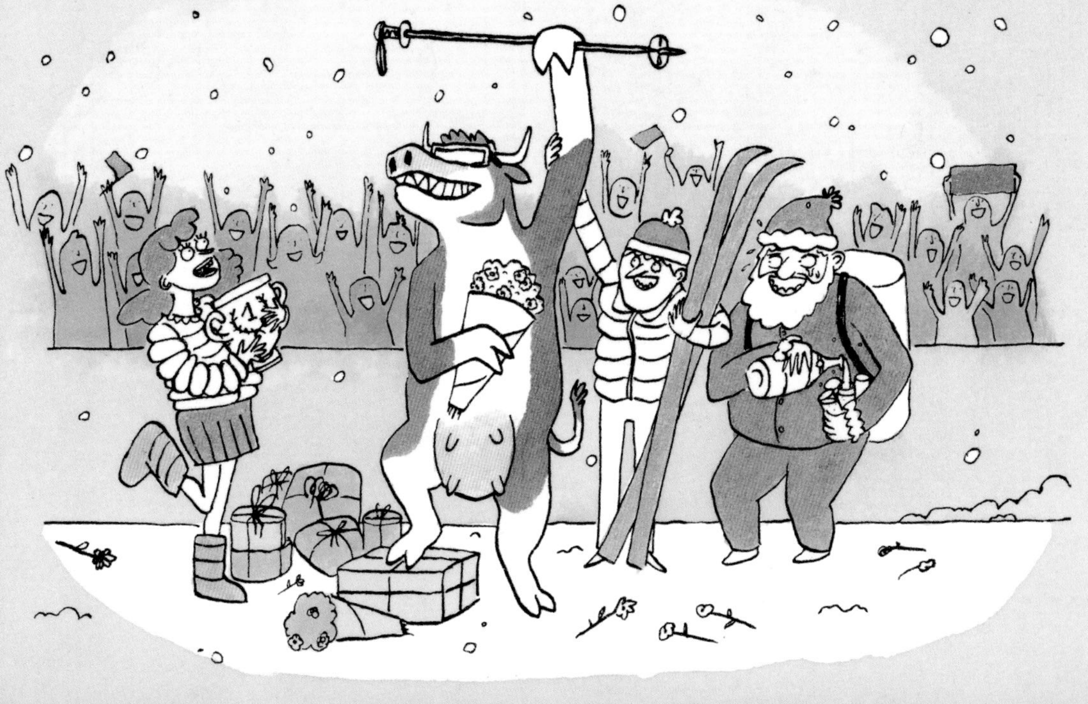

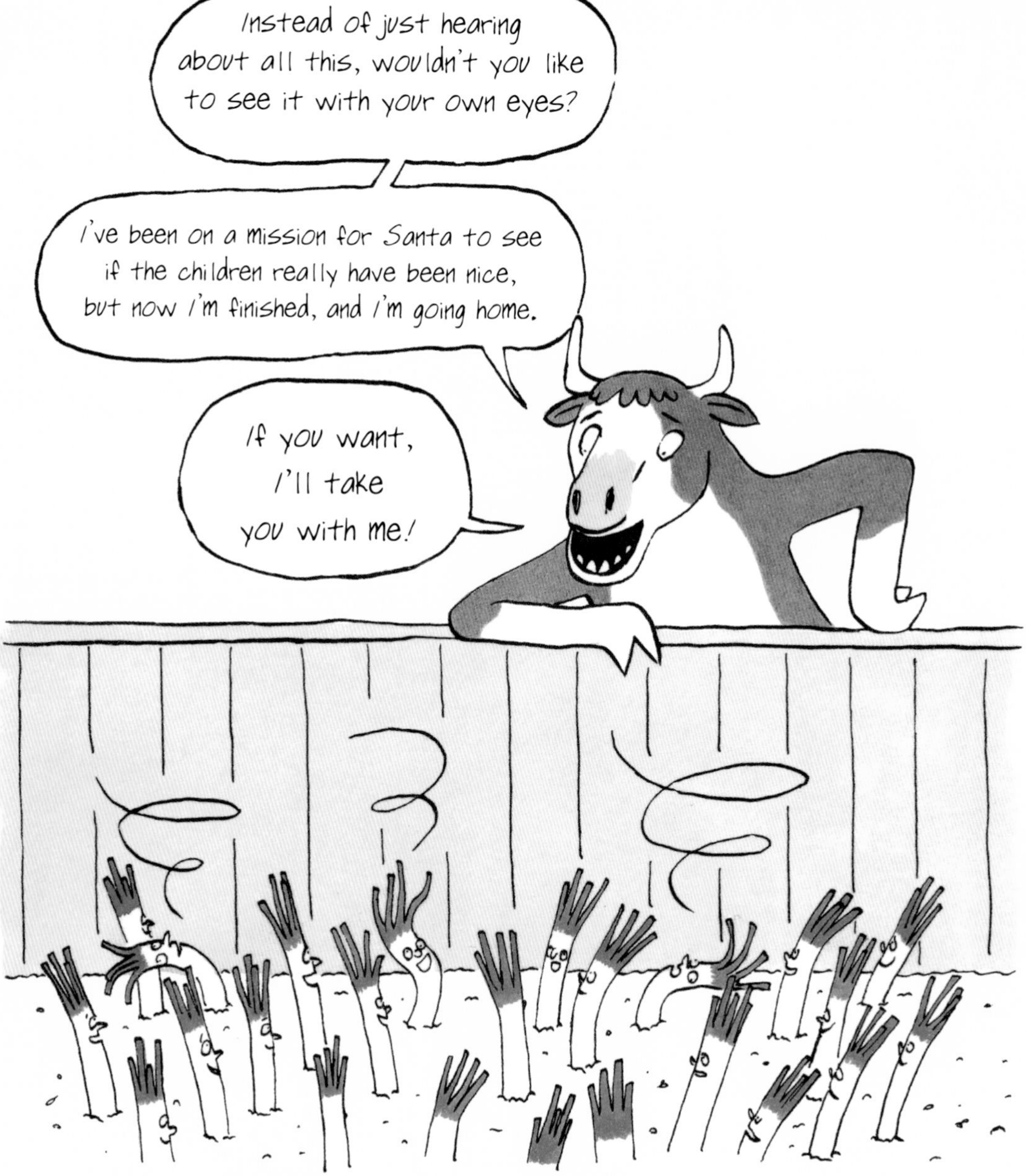
Instead of just hearing about all this, wouldn't you like to see it with your own eyes?
I've been on a mission for Santa to see if the children really have been nice, but now I'm finished, and I'm going home.
If you want, I'll take you with me!

The three emotional leeks faint again, but they revive very quickly so as not to be left behind.

We're coming to the end of the story. The leeks line up, orderly and disciplined, and one after the other they squeeze through the fence. Let's wish them a pleasant journey! They'll return from the adventure changed, no doubt . . .

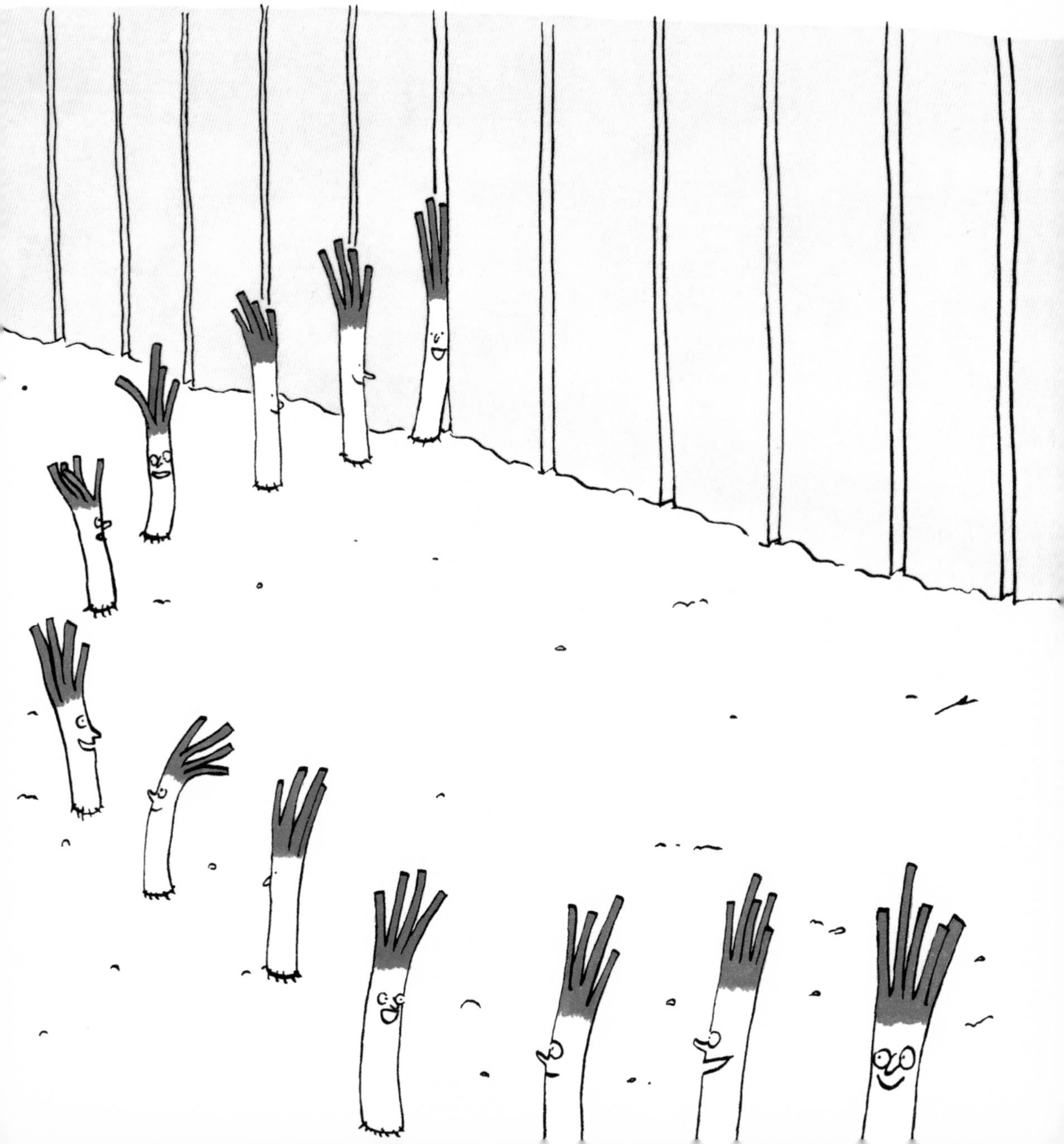

. . . if they come back at all.

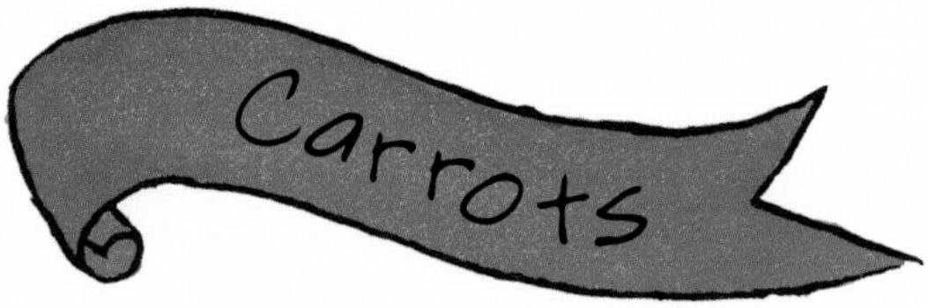
Carrots

Carrots are . . . vegetables.

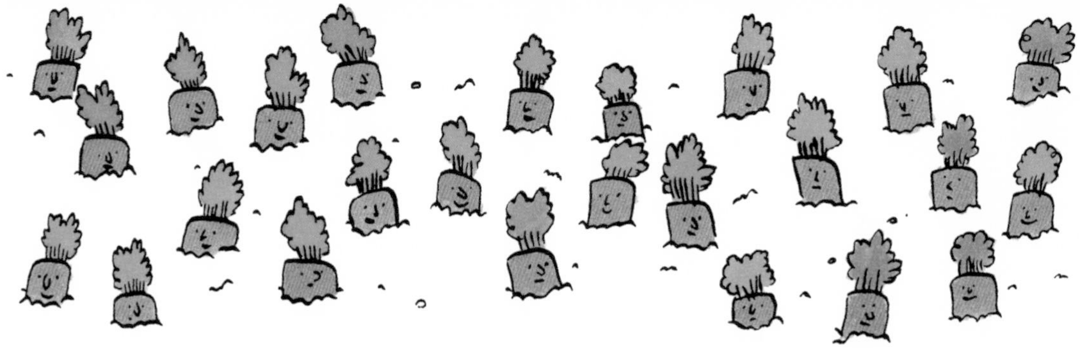

In a neighboring plot, the carrots have been following the misadventures of the leeks. At first they cracked up.

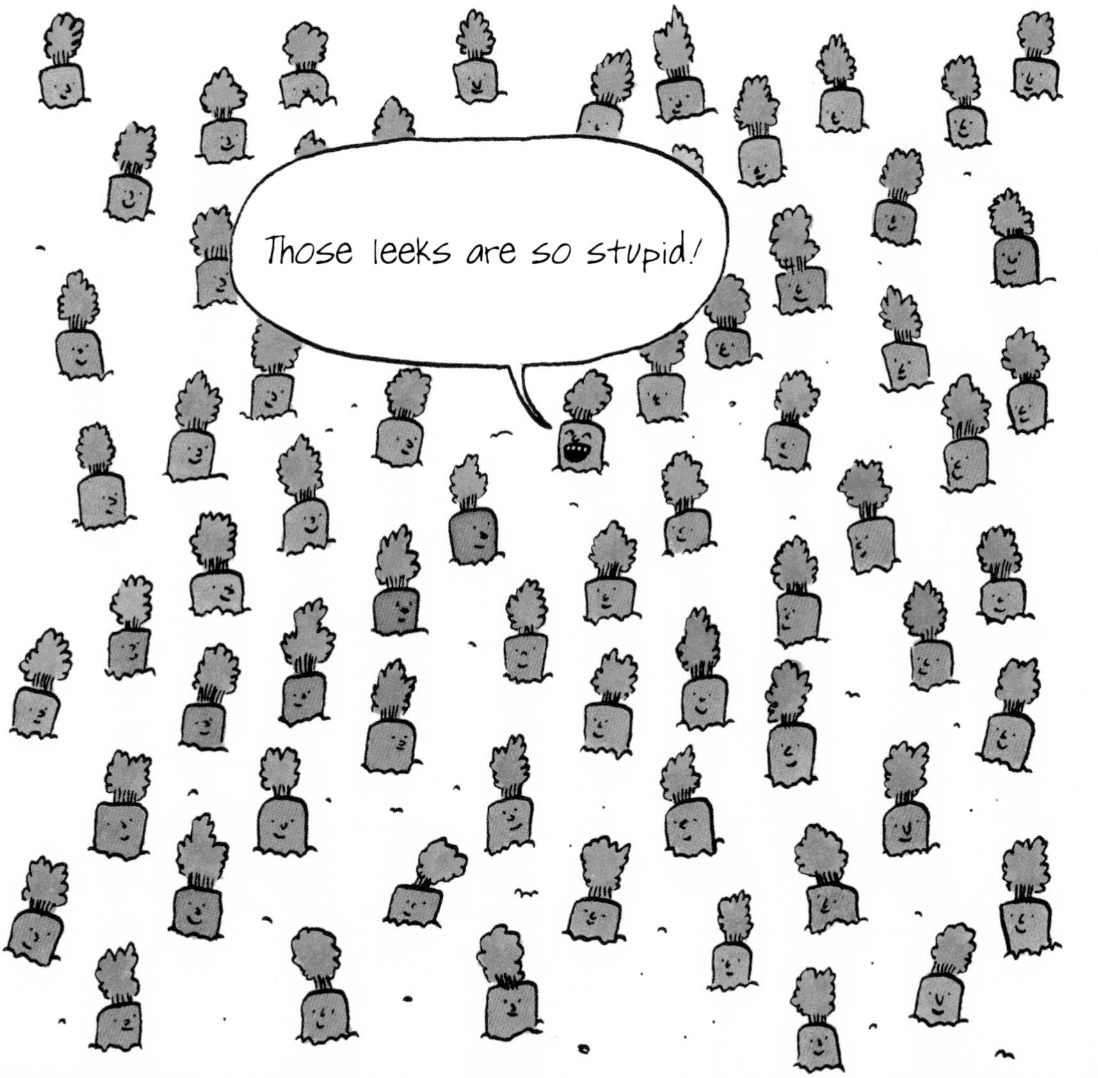
Those leeks are so stupid!

Then they began raising questions.

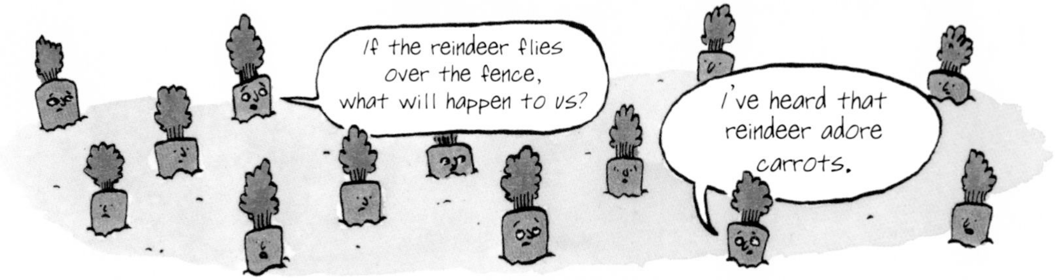
If the reindeer flies over the fence, what will happen to us?
I've heard that reindeer adore carrots.

Increasingly nervous, they start thinking about security measures.

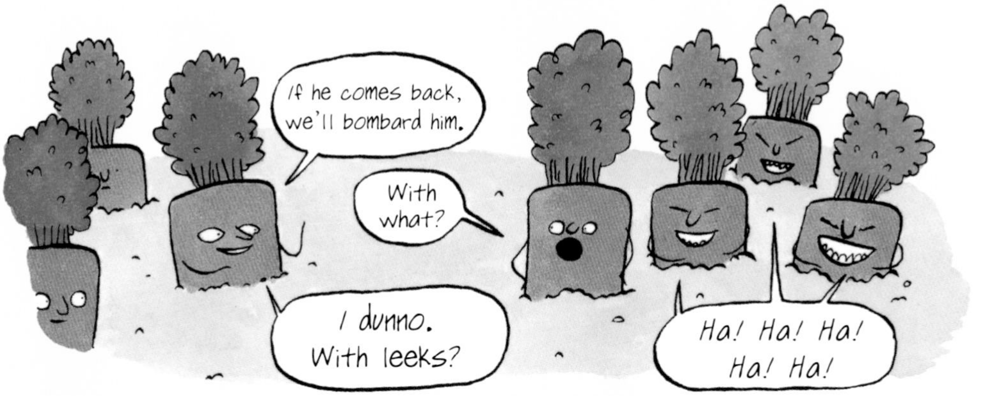
If he comes back, we'll bombard him.
With what?
I dunno. With leeks?
Ha! Ha! Ha! Ha! Ha!

The carrots have plenty of ideas, but they aren't experts in strategy.

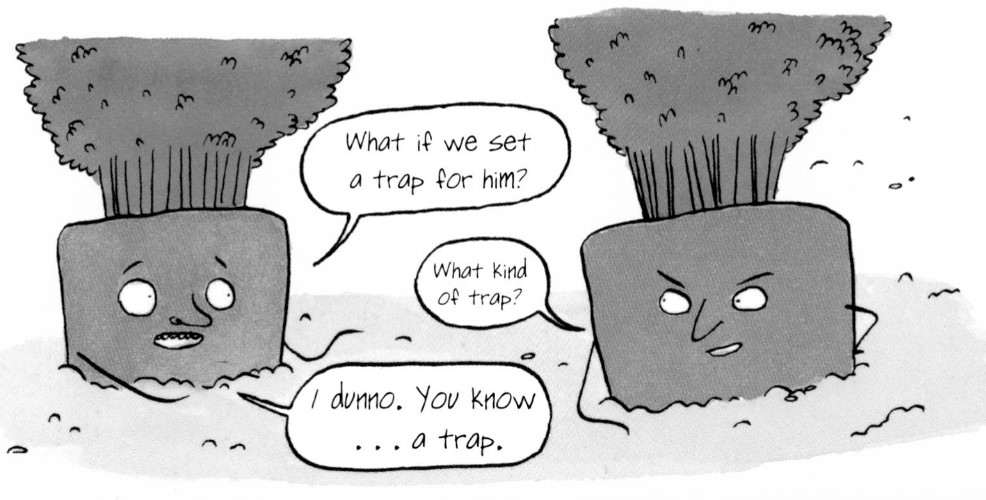
What if we set a trap for him?
What kind of trap?
I dunno. You know . . . a trap.

After several hours of discussion, everybody has forgotten the original question.

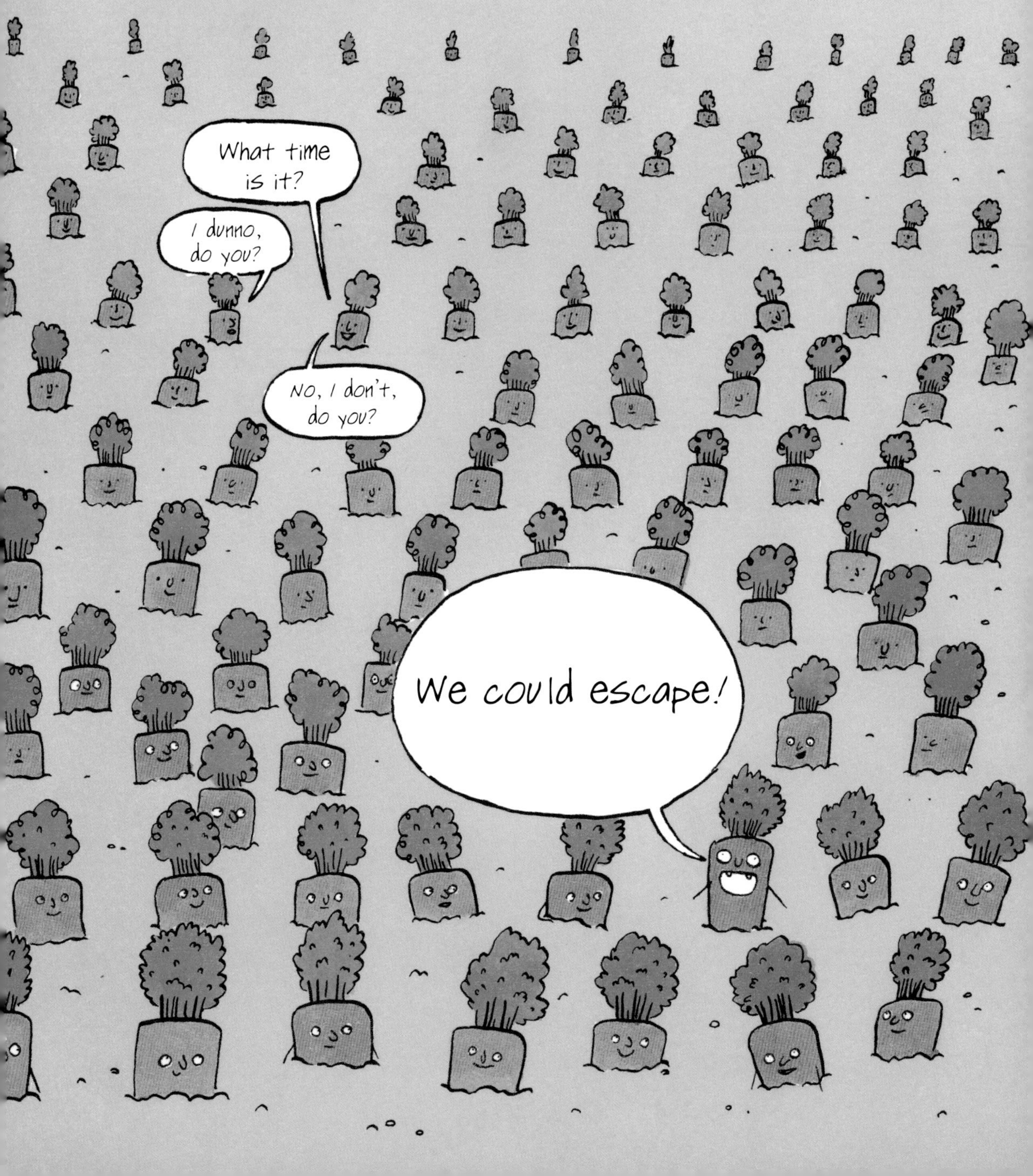
What time is it?
I dunno, do you?
No, I don't, do you?
We could escape!

Now, there's an idea!
The carrots are enthusiastic.

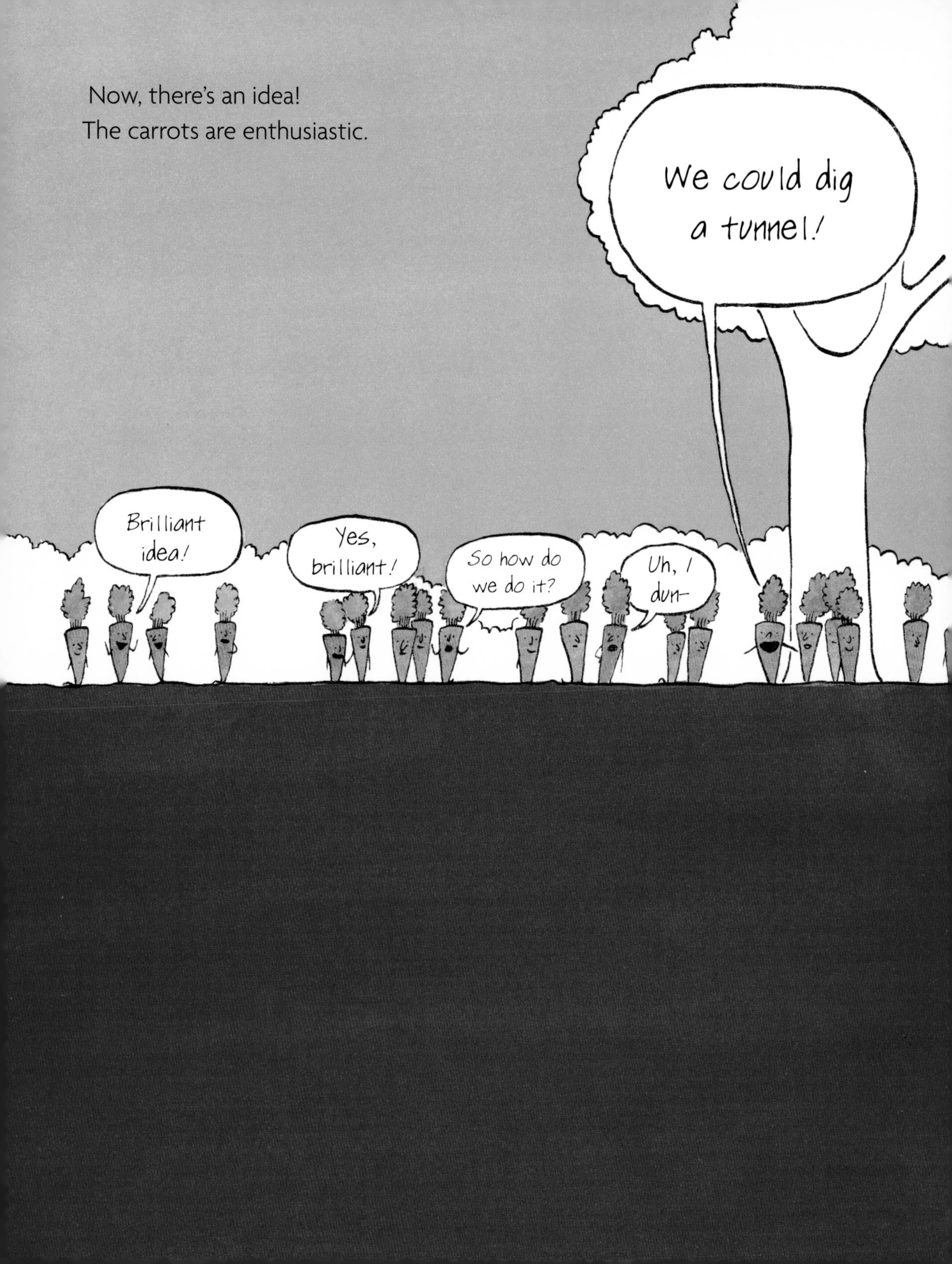
We could dig a tunnel!
Brilliant idea!
Yes, brilliant!
So how do we do it?
Uh, I dun-

Good plan! It's no sooner said than done. The carrots are experts at making holes. The one who came up with the idea is the leader, and work begins immediately. Everyone pitches in: The toughest ones dig, while the others remain on the lookout with conspiratorial expressions.

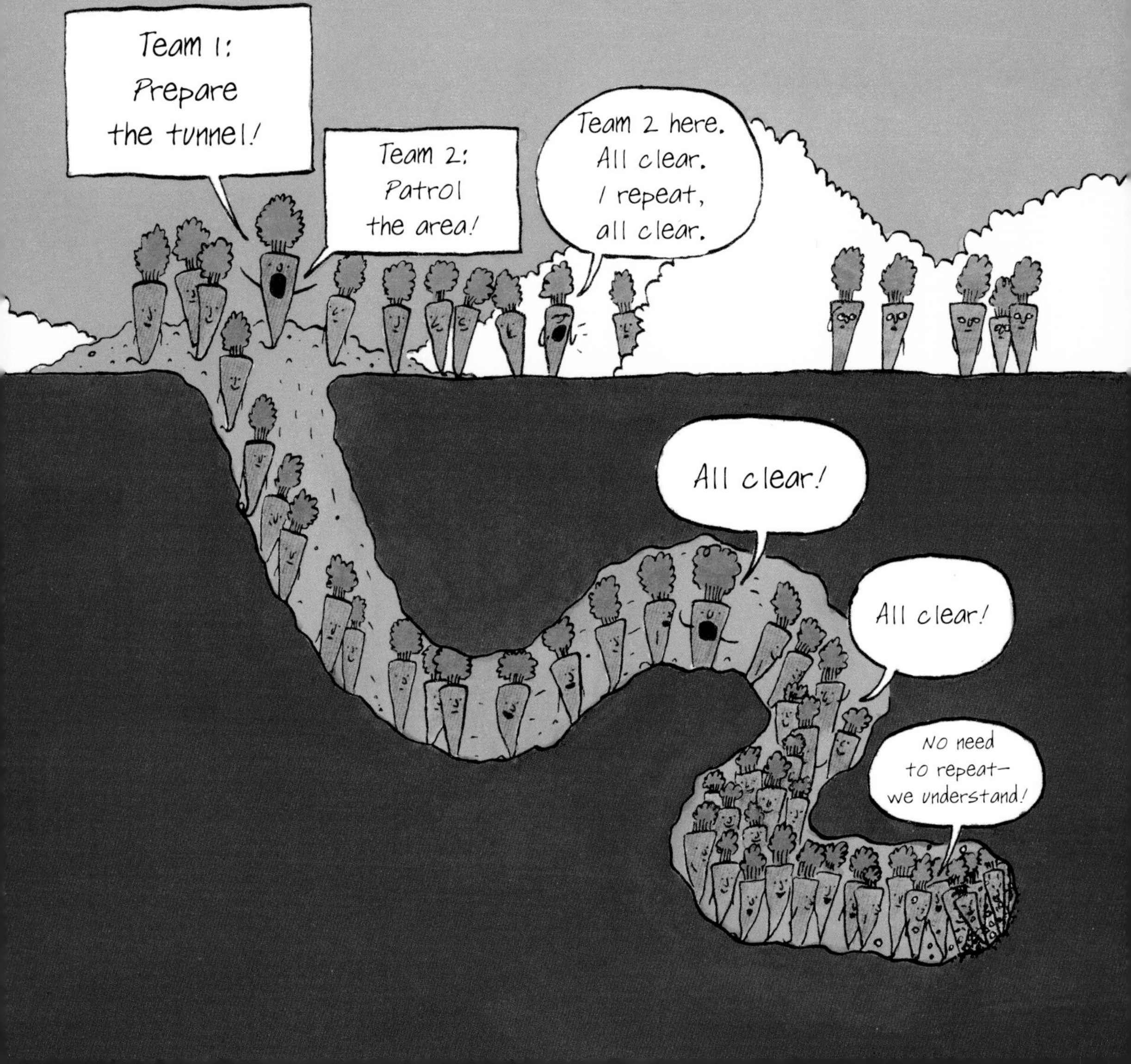

Team 1: Prepare the tunnel!
Team 2: Patrol the area!
Team 2 here. All clear. I repeat, all clear.
All clear!
All clear!
No need to repeat—we understand!

The excitement reaches its peak. With one last backward glance, everyone enters the tunnel. The leader marches at the head of the column, watching his step (except that he doesn't have feet) (but that doesn't stop him from escaping) (proof that where there's a will, there's a way).

Suddenly, the tunnel widens.
A voice above their heads says:

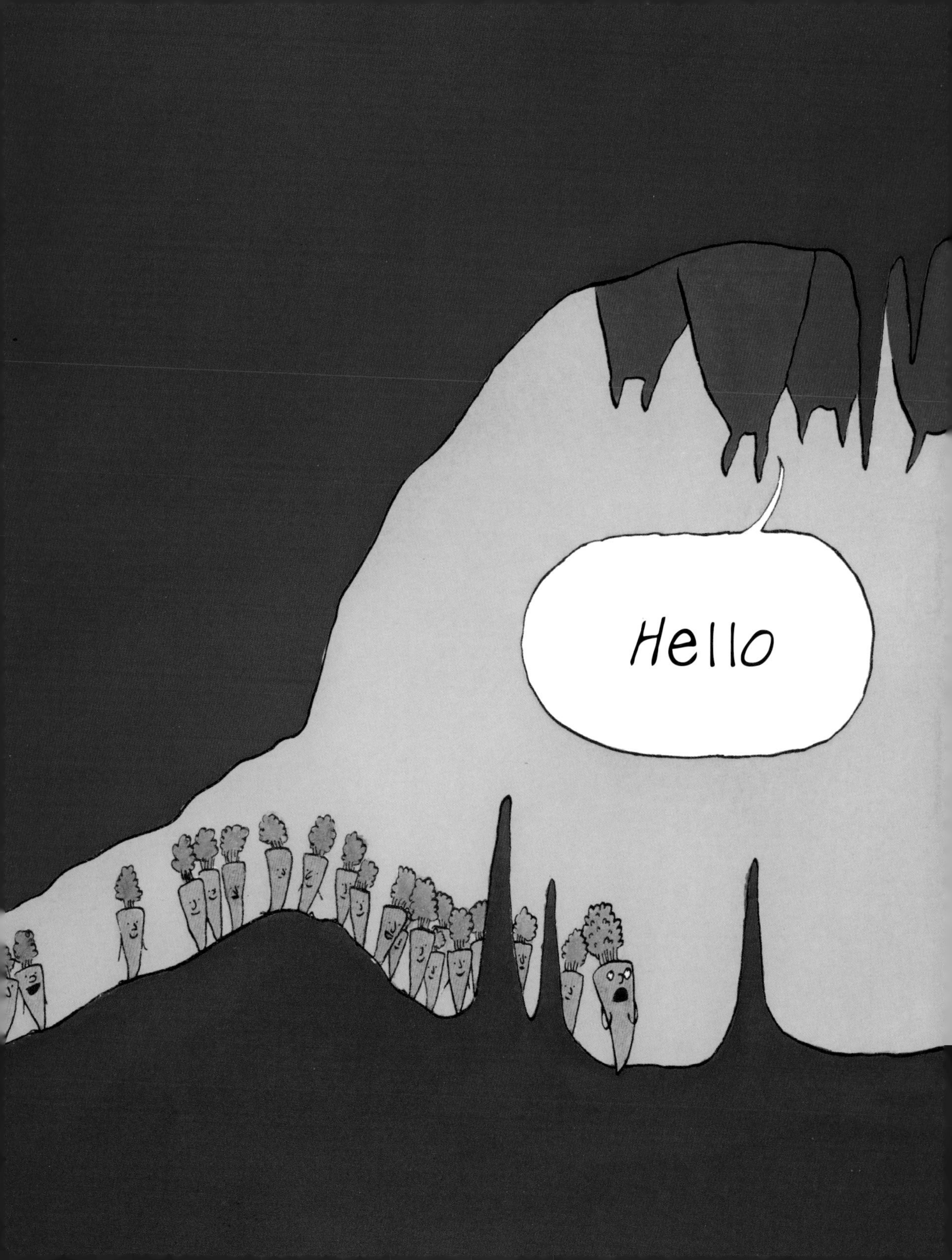
Hello

Panic among the carrots!
Who said that? Was it a
cave-dwelling reindeer?
The leader bravely takes a stand.

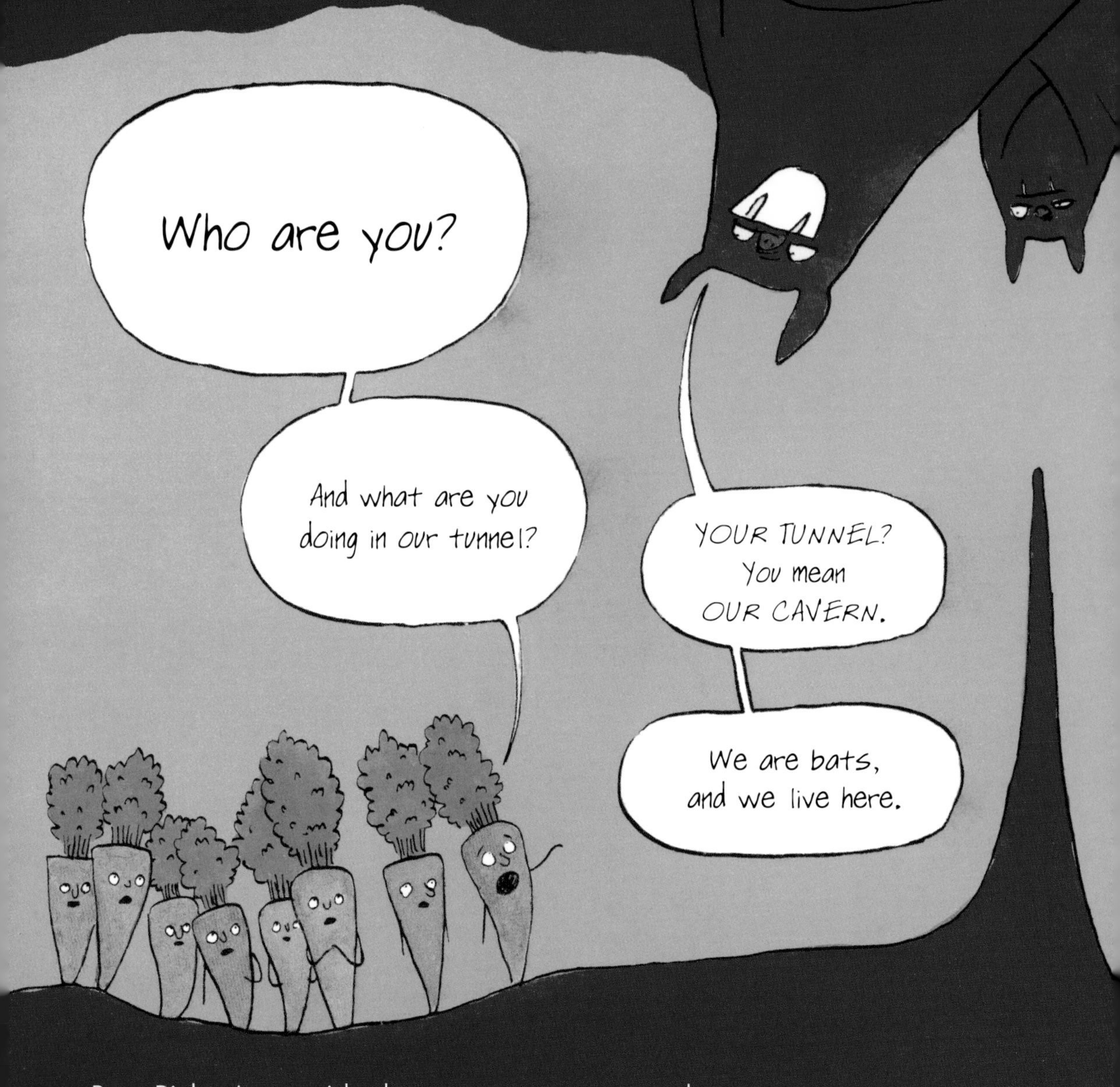

Who are you?
And what are you doing in our tunnel?
YOUR TUNNEL? You mean OUR CAVERN.
We are bats, and we live here.

Bats. Right. An anguished murmur passes among the carrots.

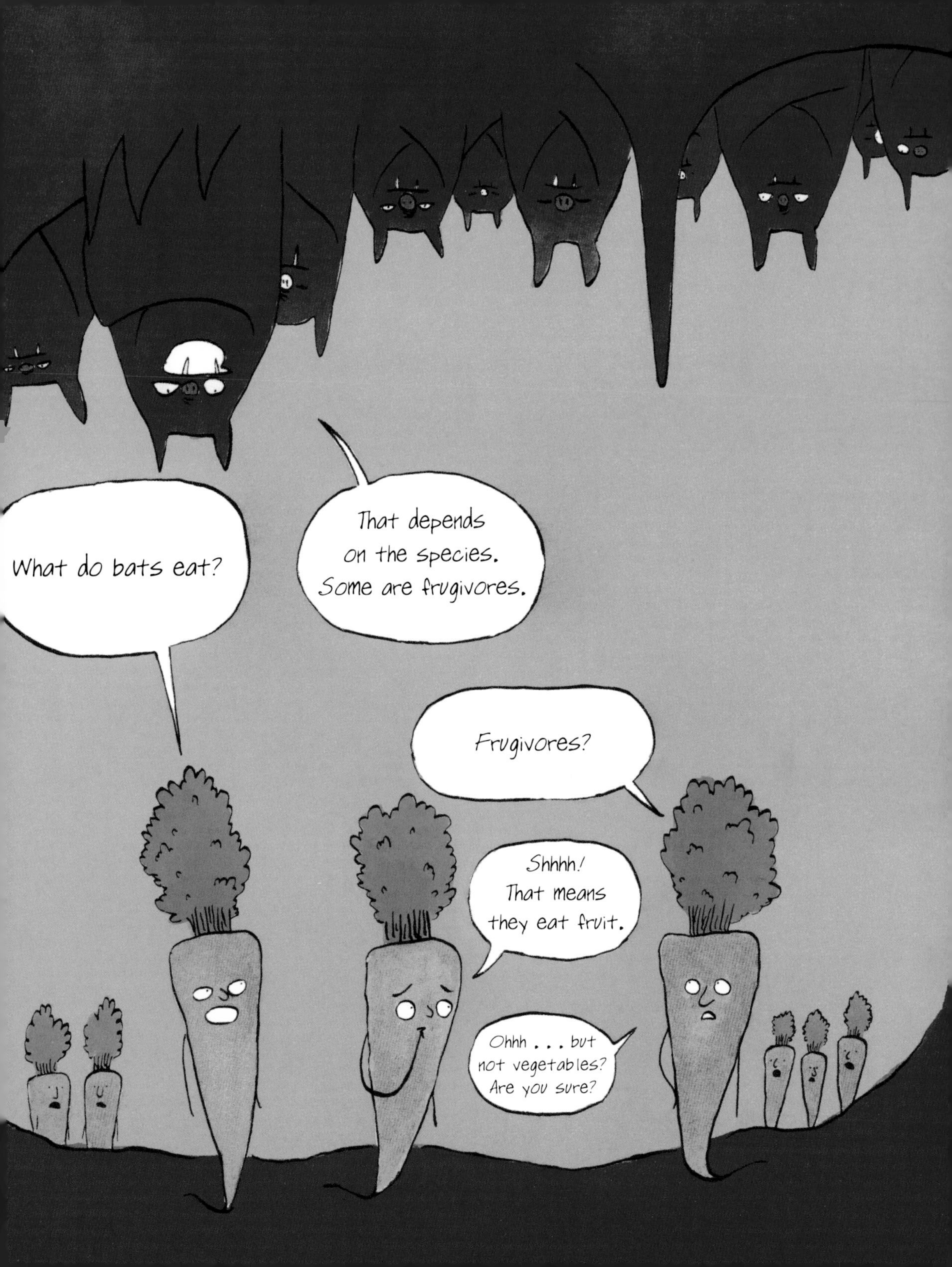
What do bats eat?
That depends on the species. Some are frugivores.
Frugivores?
Shhhh! That means they eat fruit.
Ohhh . . . but not vegetables? Are you sure?

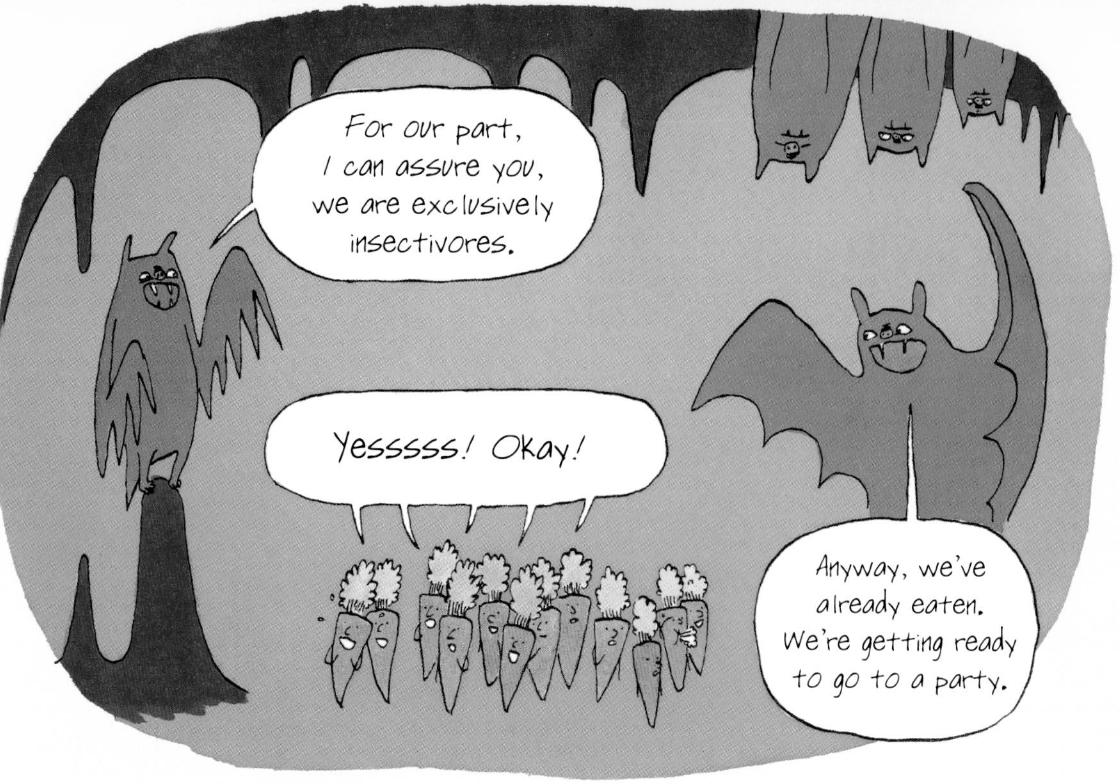
For our part, I can assure you, we are exclusively insectivores.
Yesssss! Okay!
Anyway, we've already eaten. We're getting ready to go to a party.

A party? How delightful! The carrots clap their hands (except they don't have hands) and gather around to ask for information about the occasion.

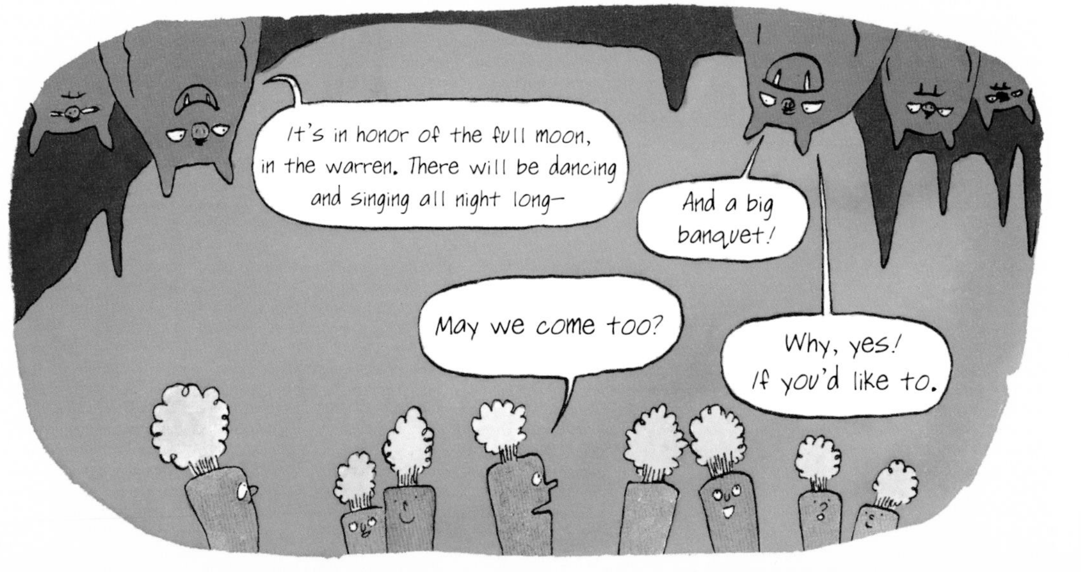
It's in honor of the full moon, in the warren. There will be dancing and singing all night long—
And a big banquet!
May we come too?
Why, yes! If you'd like to.

Could there be a better way for carrots to start a new life than to take advantage of their hard-won freedom?

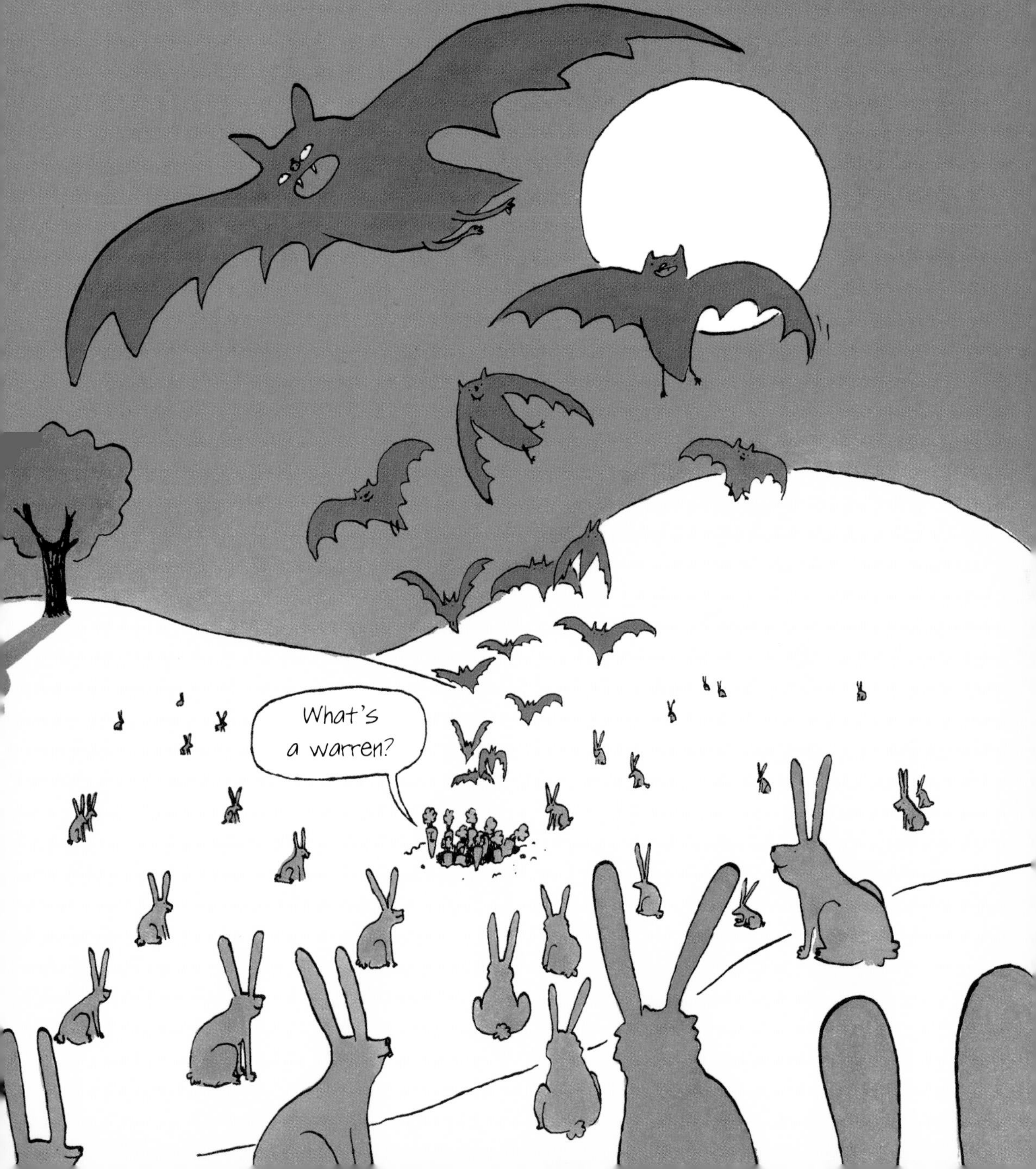
What's a warren?

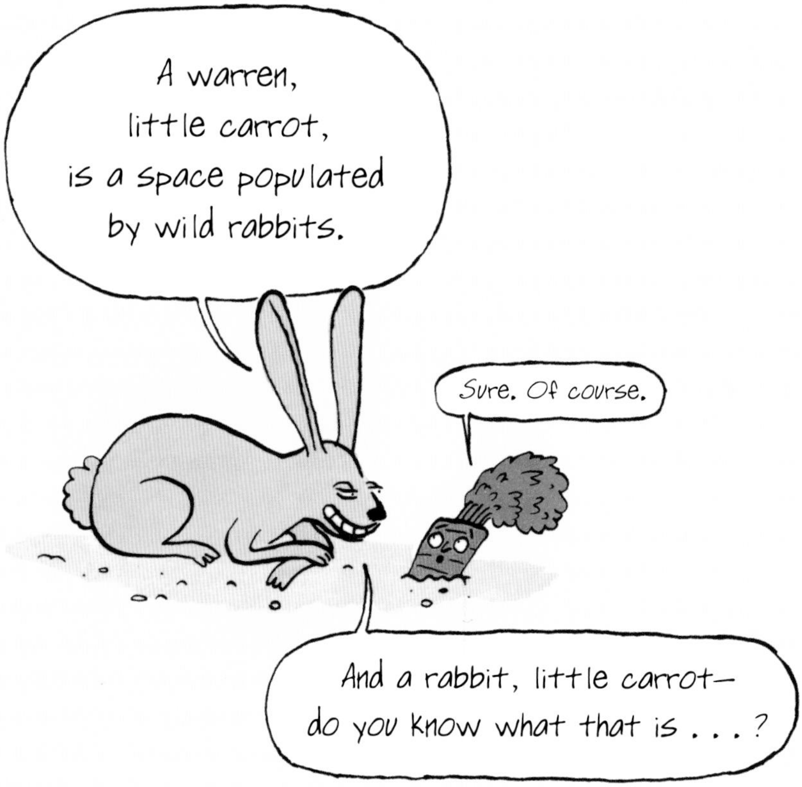
A warren, little carrot, is a space populated by wild rabbits.
Sure. Of course.
And a rabbit, little carrot— do you know what that is . . . ?

Mixed Vegetables

The two preceding stories, dear reader, are exceptional episodes from life in the vegetable garden. The great majority of leeks and carrots grow without drama. They even take a certain pride in that.

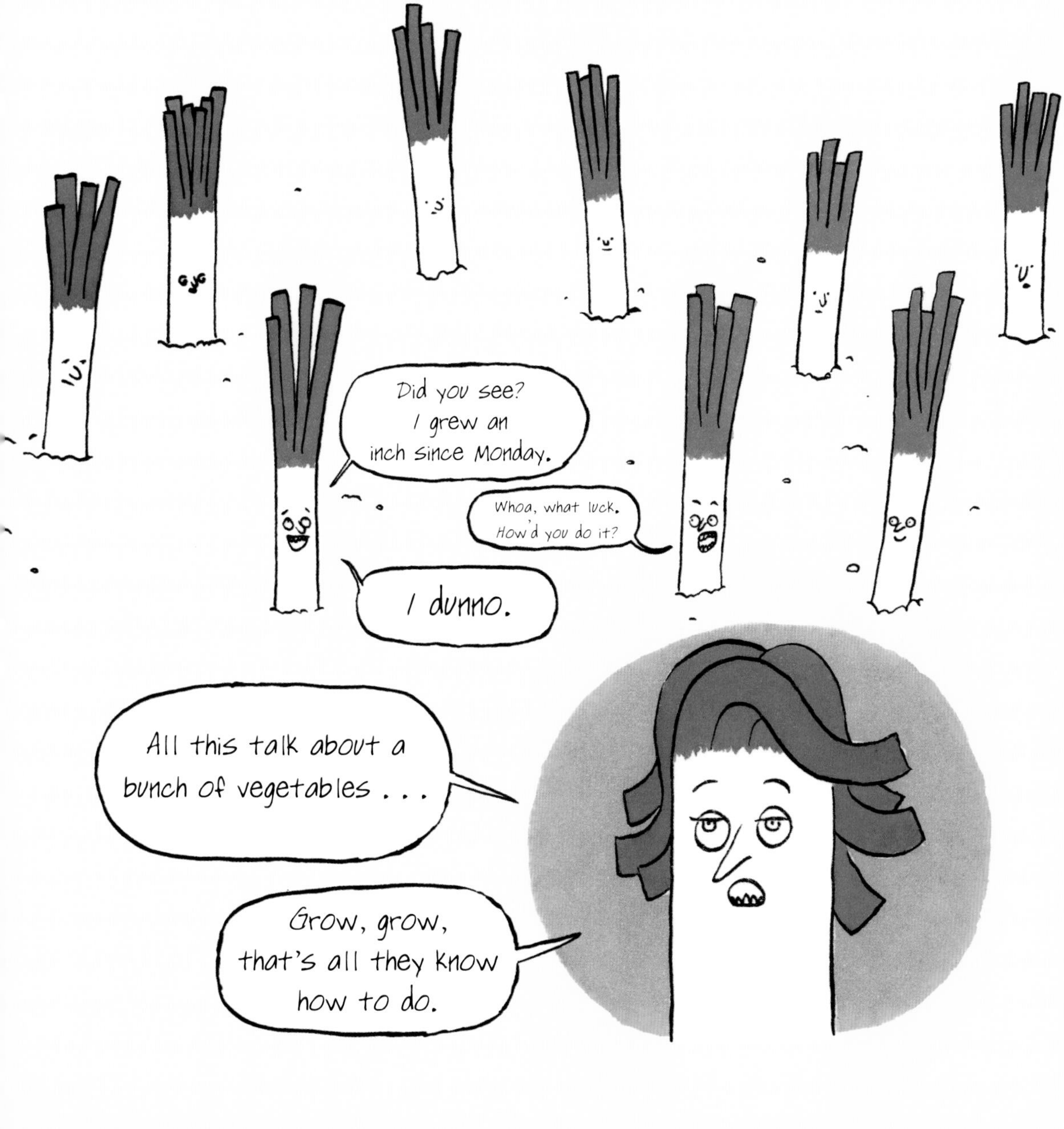
Did you see? I grew an inch since Monday.
Whoa, what luck. How'd you do it?
I dunno.
All this talk about a bunch of vegetables . . .
Grow, grow, that's all they know how to do.

Romeo is a leek with a difference. A rebellious lock sweeps across his mysterious forehead.

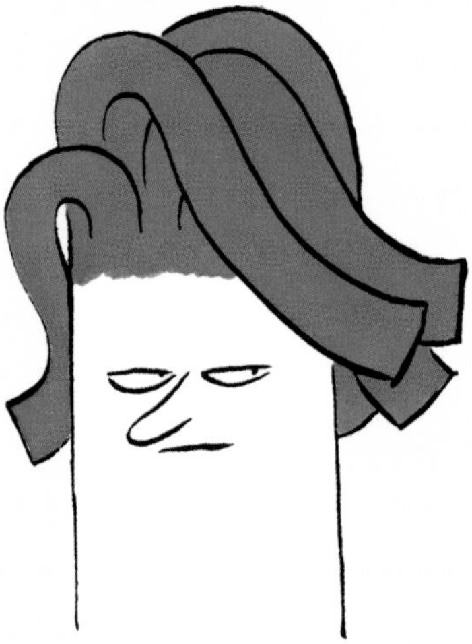

At night, when the others are asleep, he leaves the leek patch and ascends a ladder.

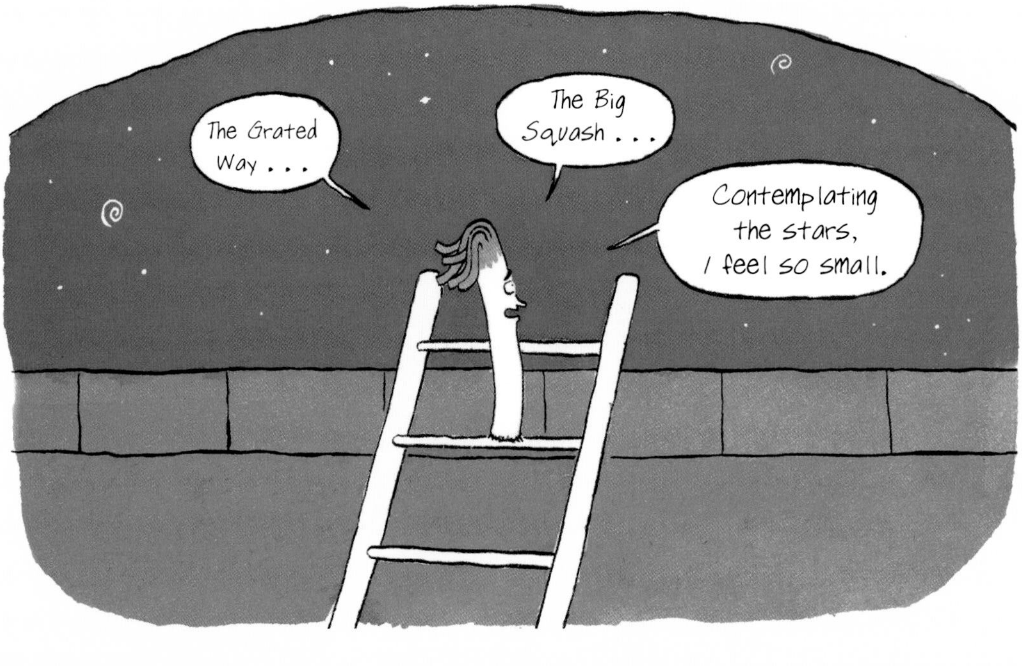
The Grated Way . . .
The Big Squash . . .
Contemplating the stars, I feel so small.

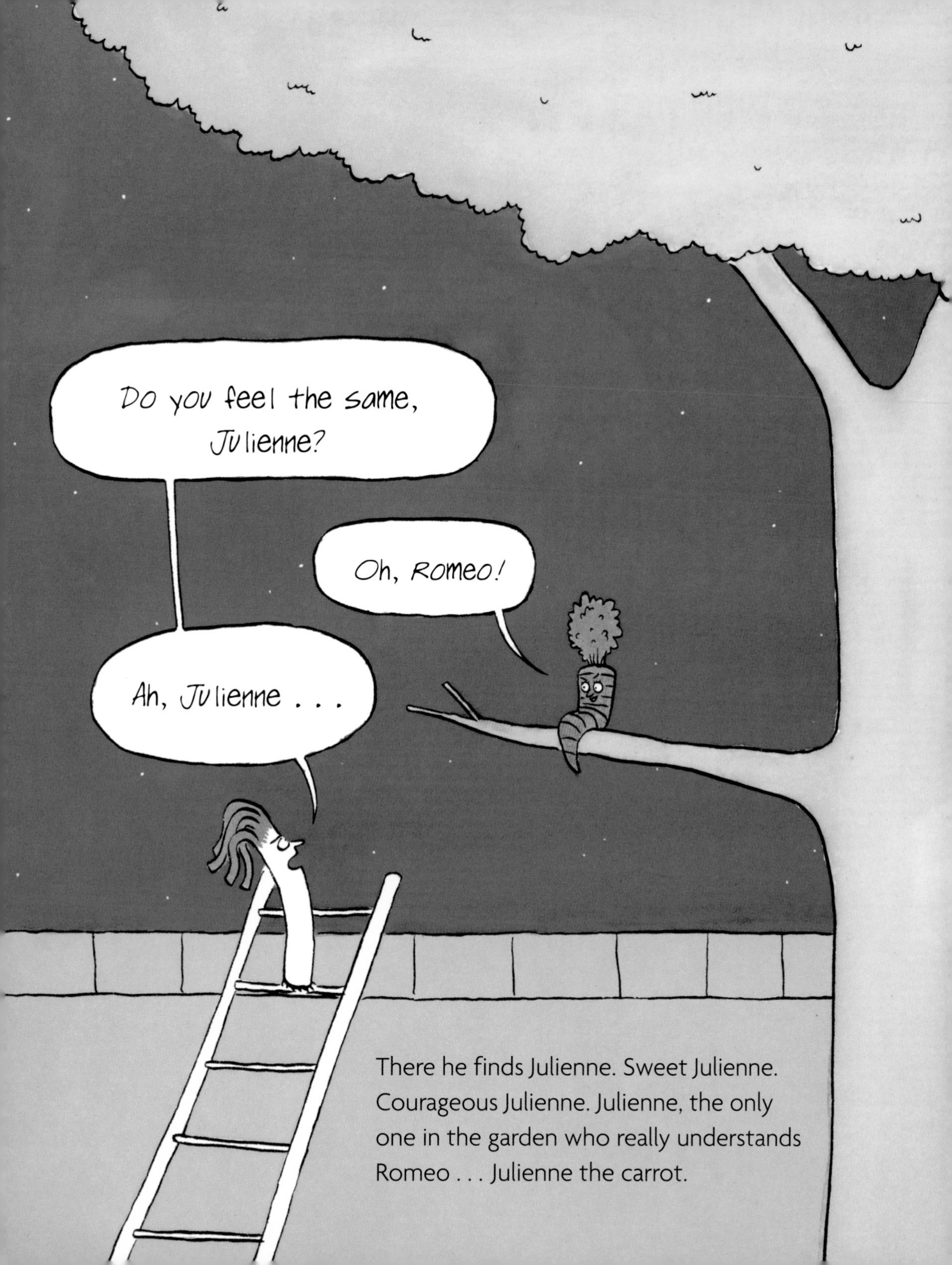
Do you feel the same, Julienne?
Oh, Romeo!
Ah, Julienne . . .

There he finds Julienne. Sweet Julienne. Courageous Julienne. Julienne, the only one in the garden who really understands Romeo . . . Julienne the carrot.

And that's a problem. In the garden, mixing with other families is discouraged. The leeks stay with the leeks, the carrots with the carrots, the radishes with the radishes—that's just the way it is. So it's a big secret that Romeo and Julienne meet at nightfall. They gaze at the stars and whisper tenderly until dawn.

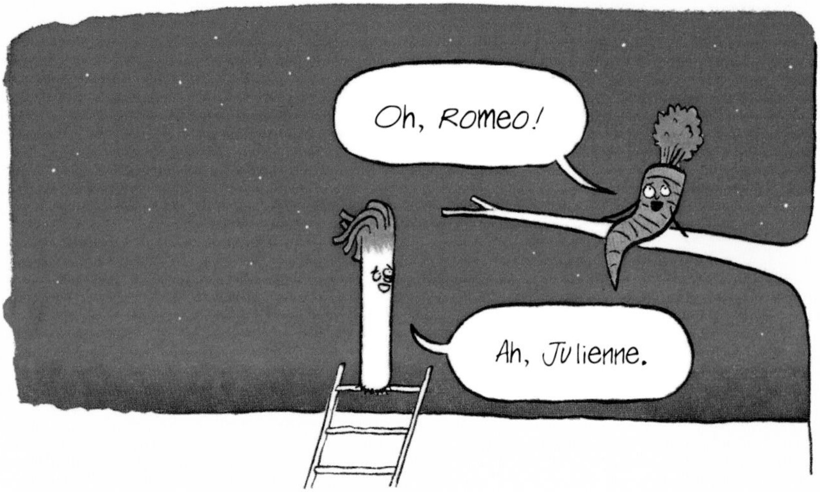

Oh, Romeo!
Ah, Julienne.

But one day, the inevitable occurs. As they are saying goodbye after a night of tender whispering, they are surprised by a patrol. Make that two patrols.

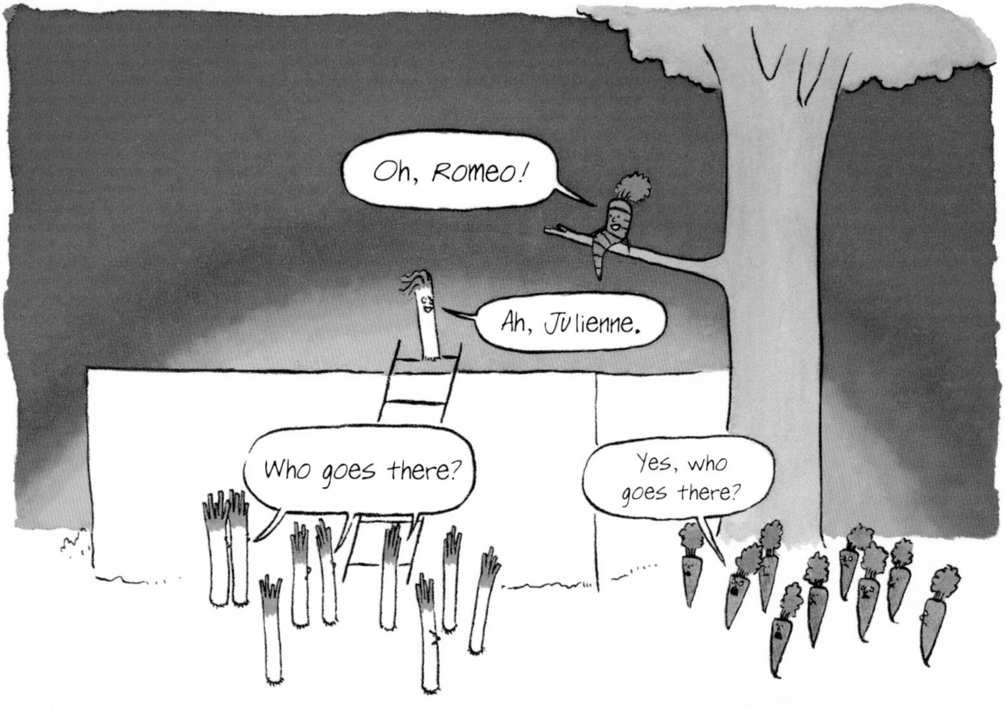

Oh, Romeo!
Ah, Julienne.
Who goes there?
Yes, who goes there?

Soon the whole garden knows about it. What a scandal! A crowd gathers—leeks on one side, carrots on the other—and insults begin to fly.

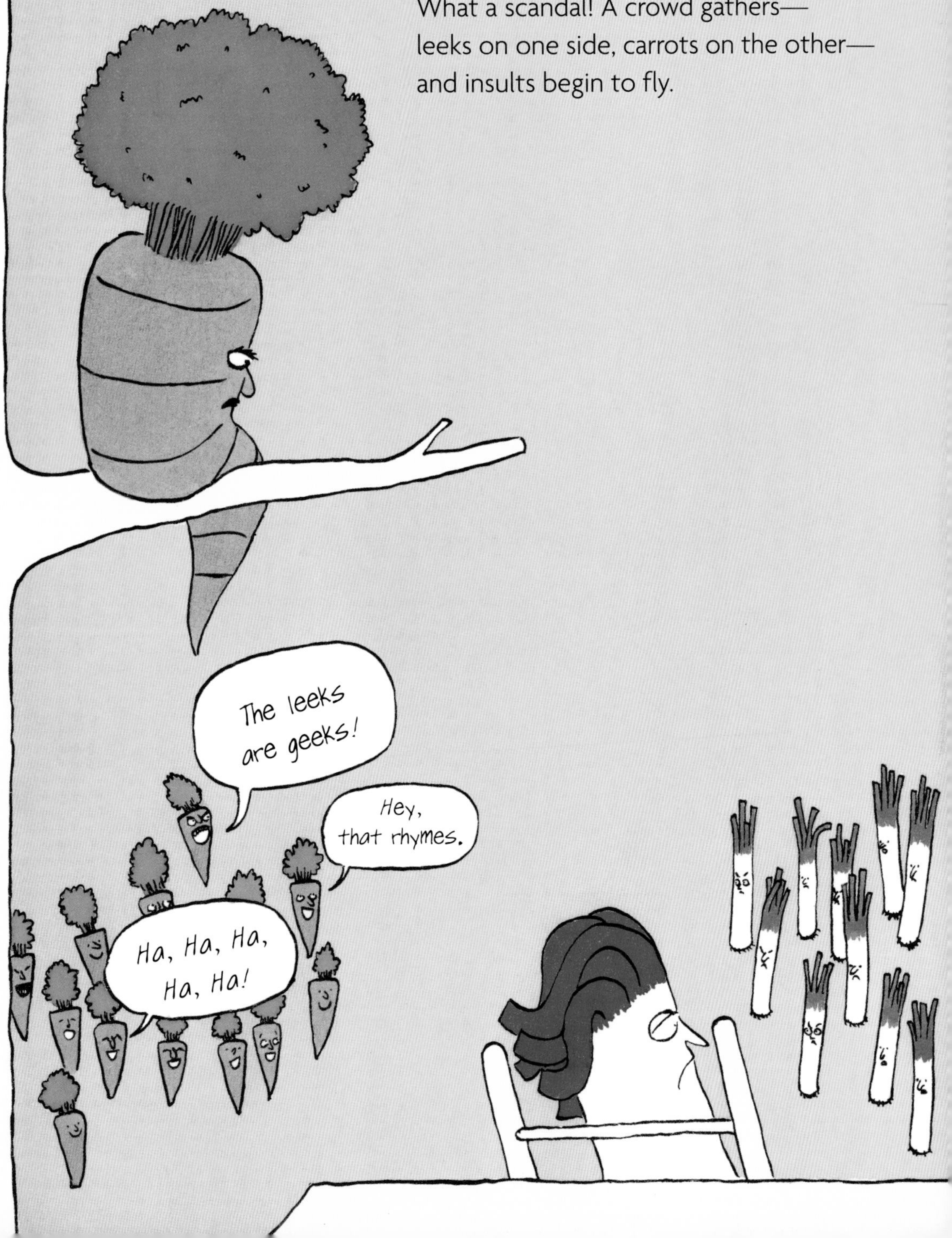
The leeks are geeks!
Hey, that rhymes.
Ha, Ha, Ha, Ha, Ha!

It escalates. Clearly, the two families have a lot to talk about.

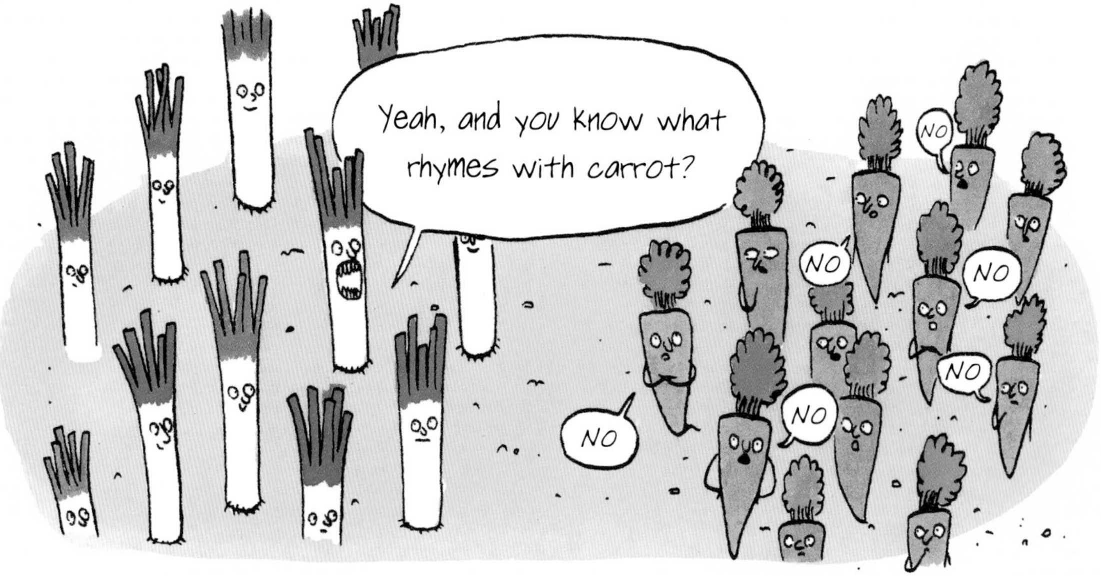
Yeah, and you know what rhymes with carrot?
NO
NO
NO
NO
NO
NO

Perhaps they were only waiting for an excuse. Romeo and Julienne are already forgotten.

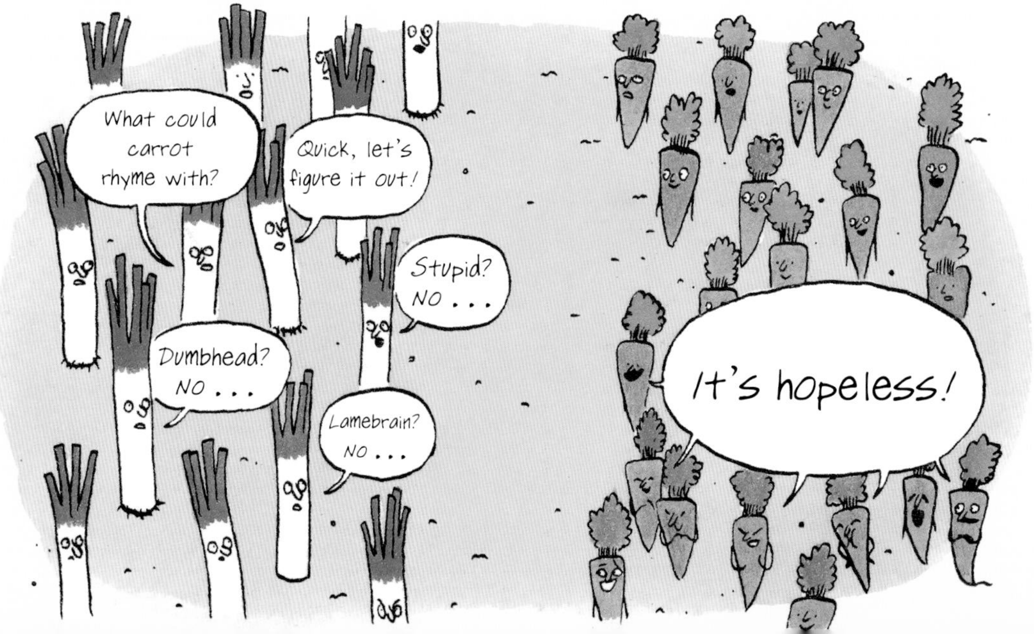
What could carrot rhyme with?
Quick, let's figure it out!
Stupid? NO . . .
Dumbhead? NO . . .
Lamebrain? NO . . .
It's hopeless!

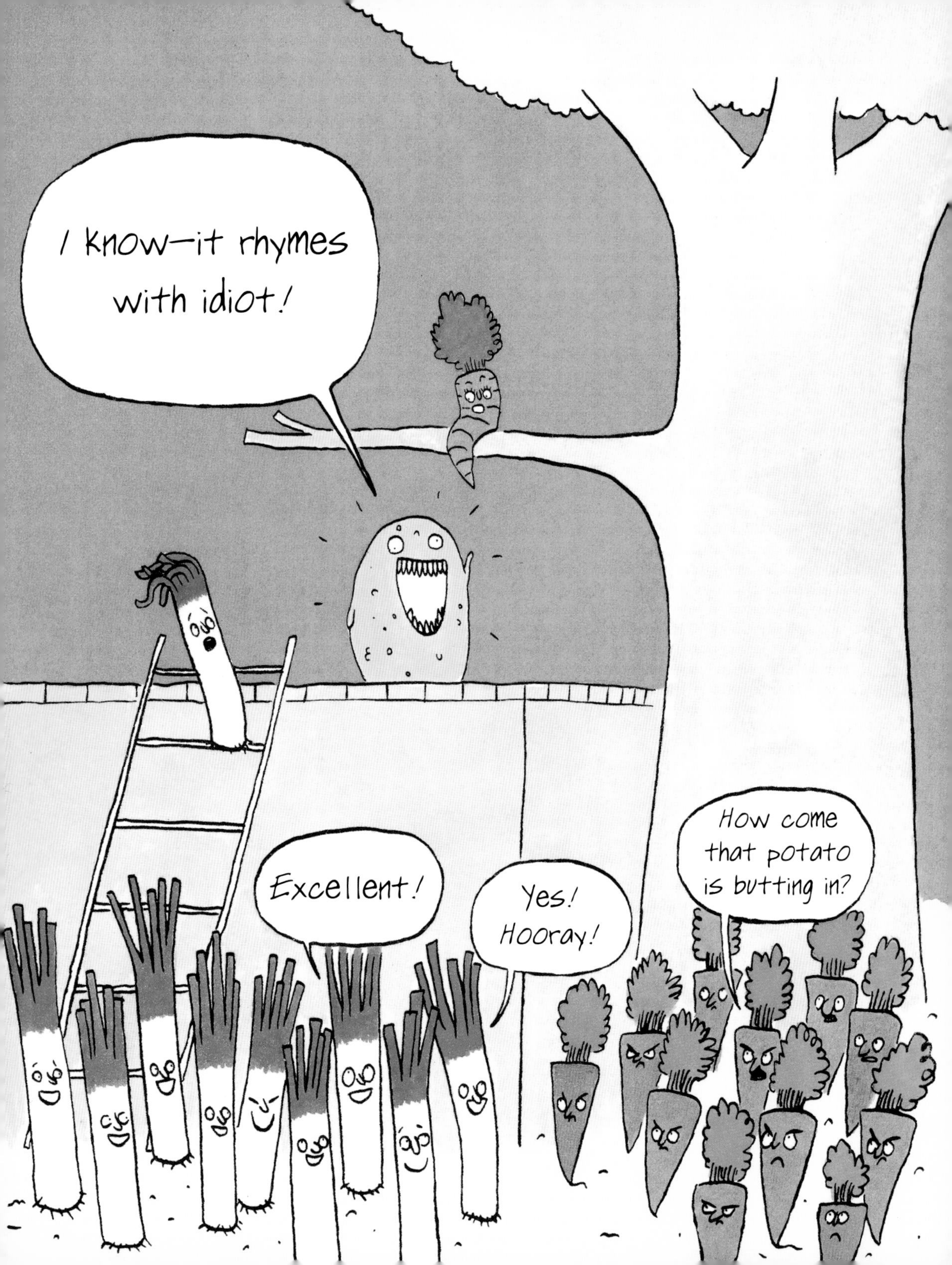
I know—it rhymes with idiot!
Excellent!
Yes! Hooray!
How come that potato is butting in?

It takes almost nothing—a potato, as it happens—to make the situation deteriorate and the most reasonable vegetables forsake their good manners.

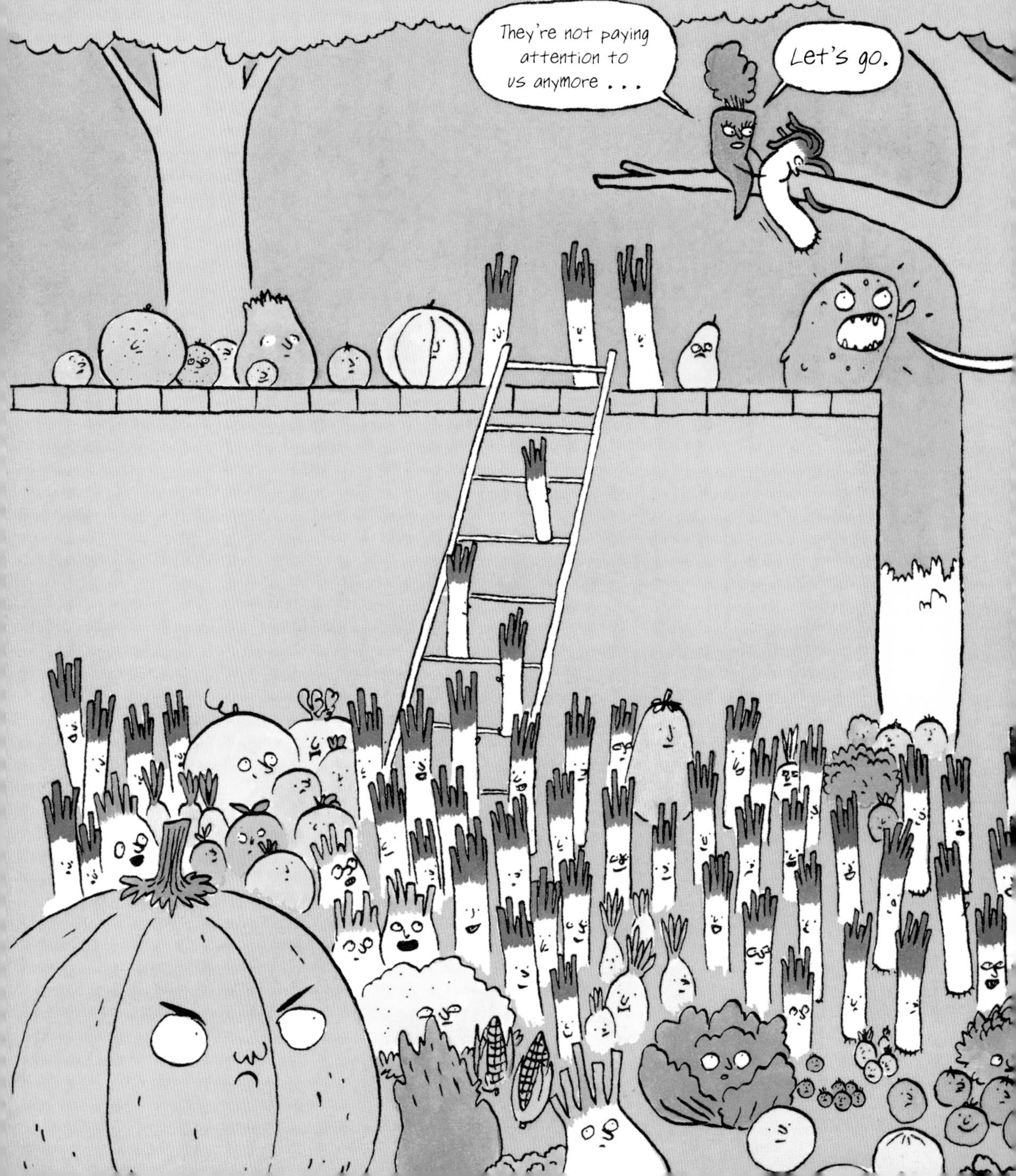
They're not paying attention to us anymore . . .
Let's go.

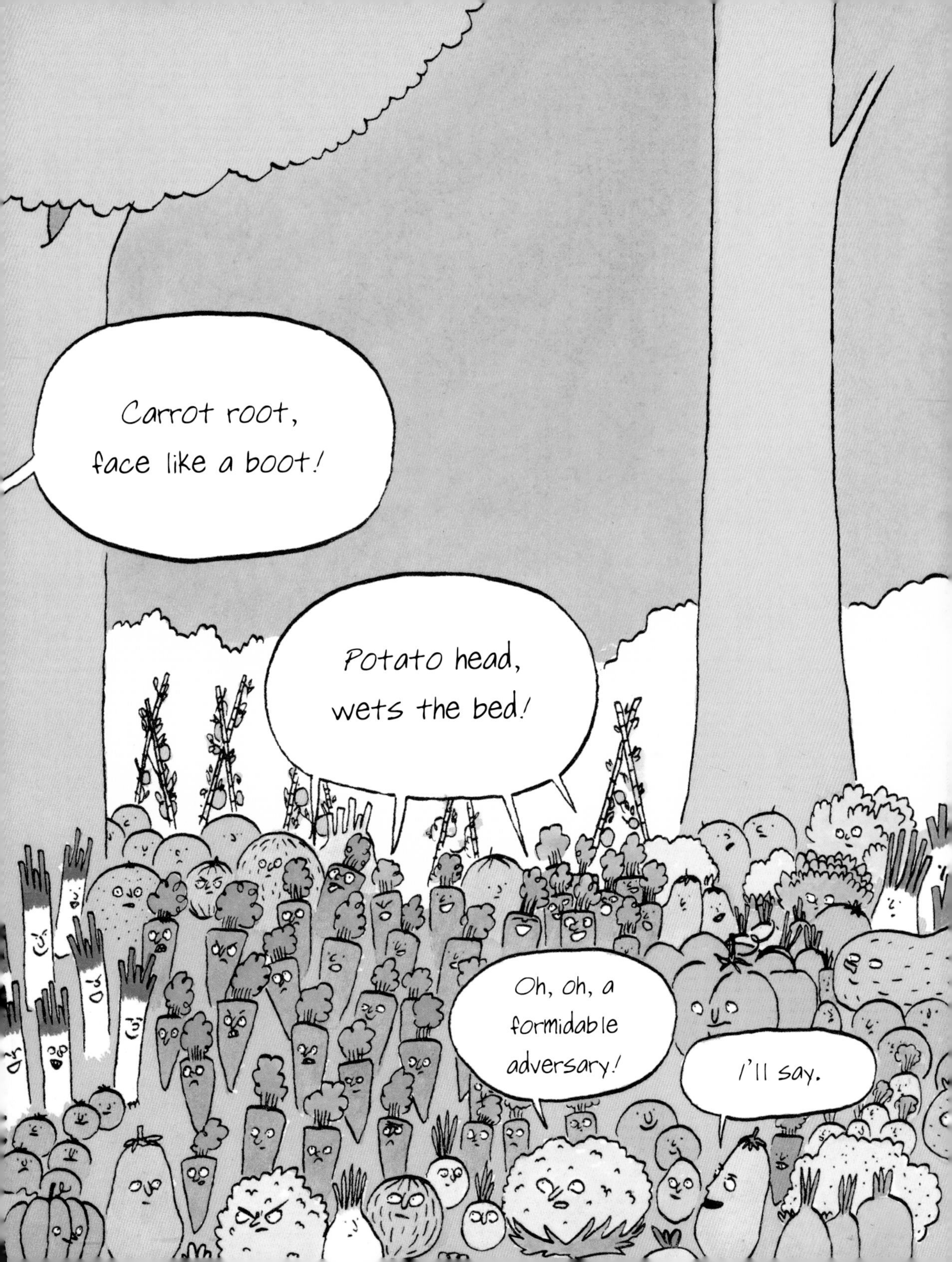

Carrot root, face like a boot!
Potato head, wets the bed!
Oh, oh, a formidable adversary!
I'll say.

Inevitably, they start throwing punches (so to speak).

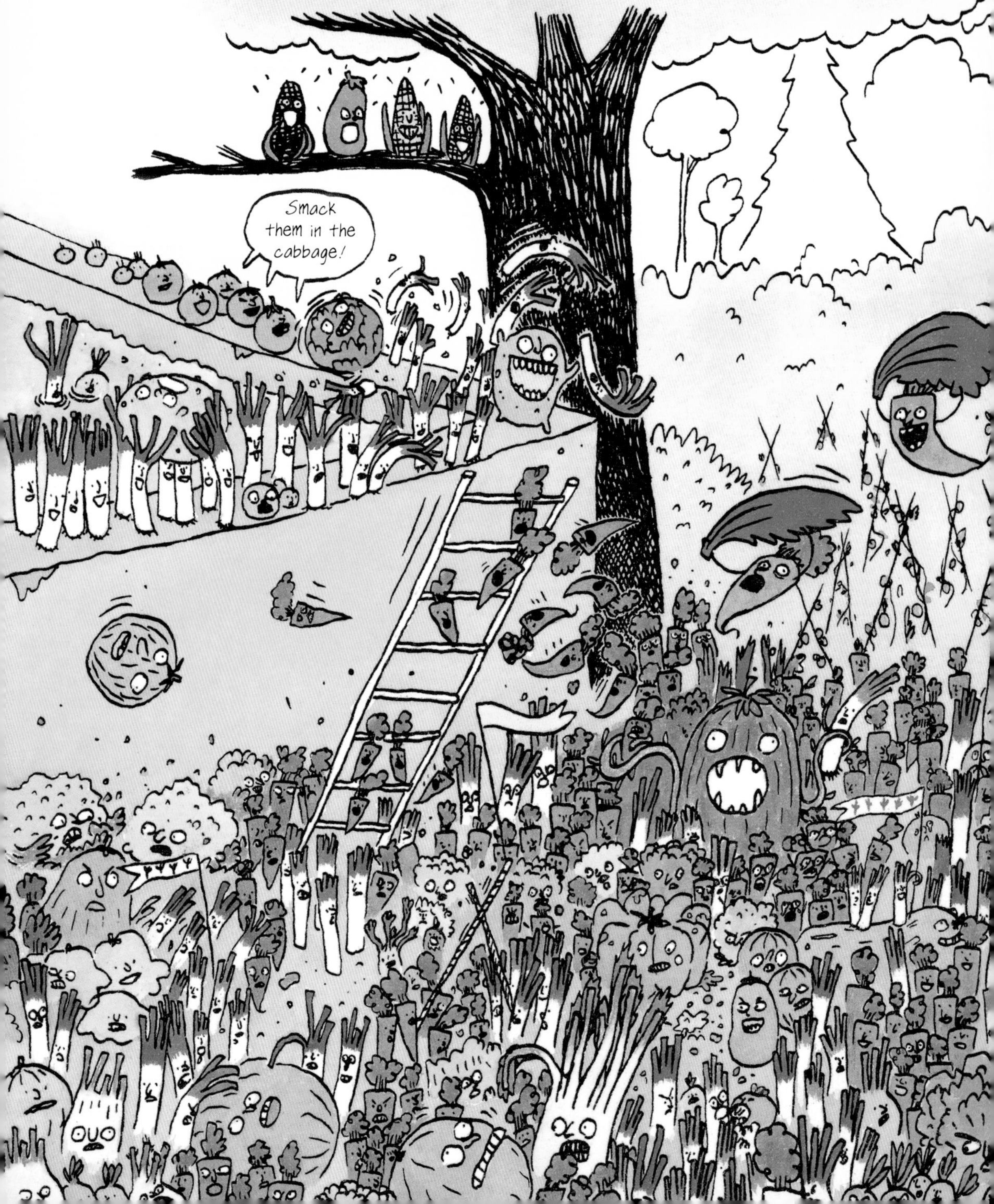
Smack them in the cabbage!

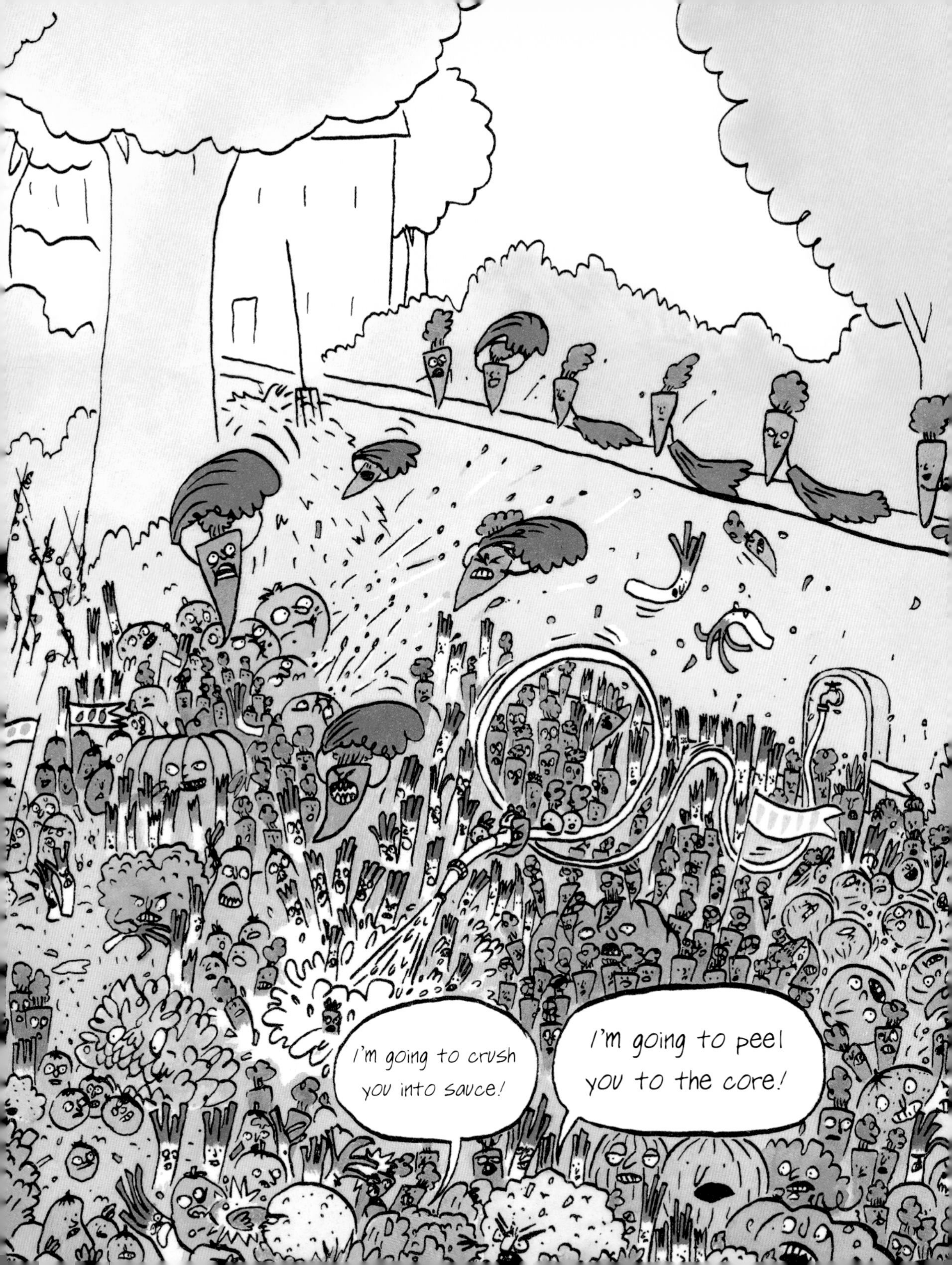
I'm going to crush you into sauce!
I'm going to peel you to the core!

The conclusion . . .

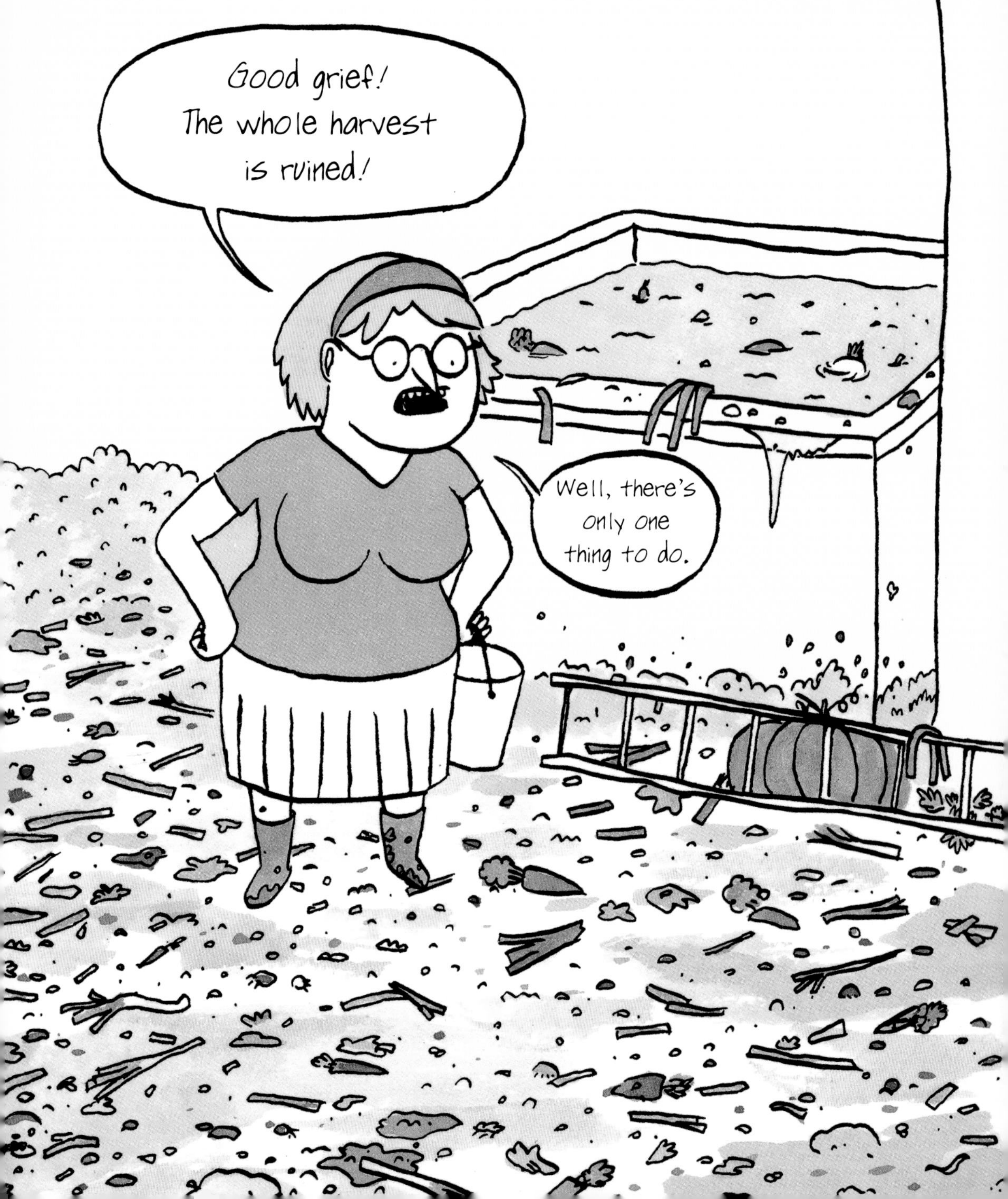
Good grief! The whole harvest is ruined!
Well, there's only one thing to do.

Here are some valuable lessons to take away:

Violence is not the answer.

There's no point in trying to grow fast. Take your time.

In the vegetable garden, everything winds up as soup.

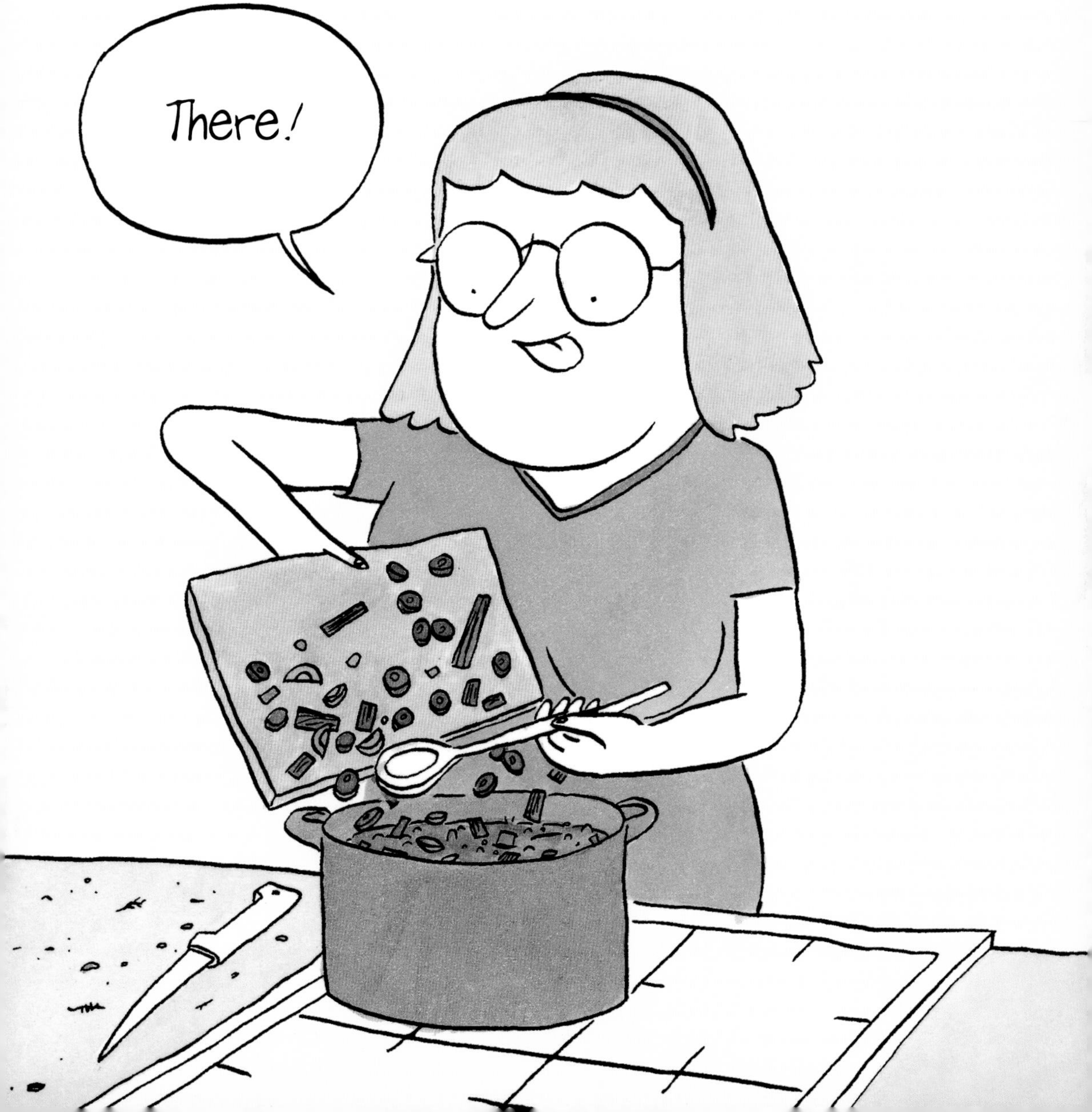
There!

And love always triumphs.

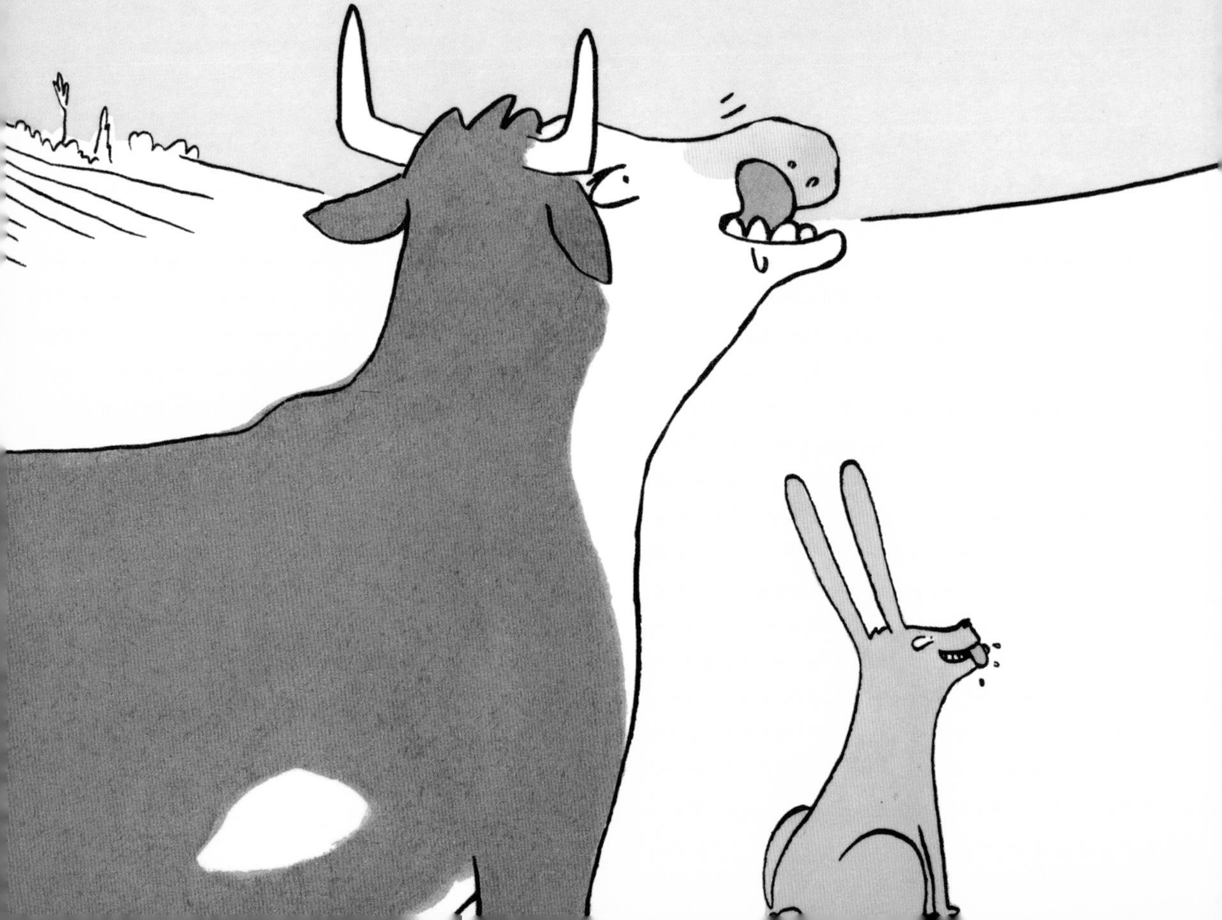

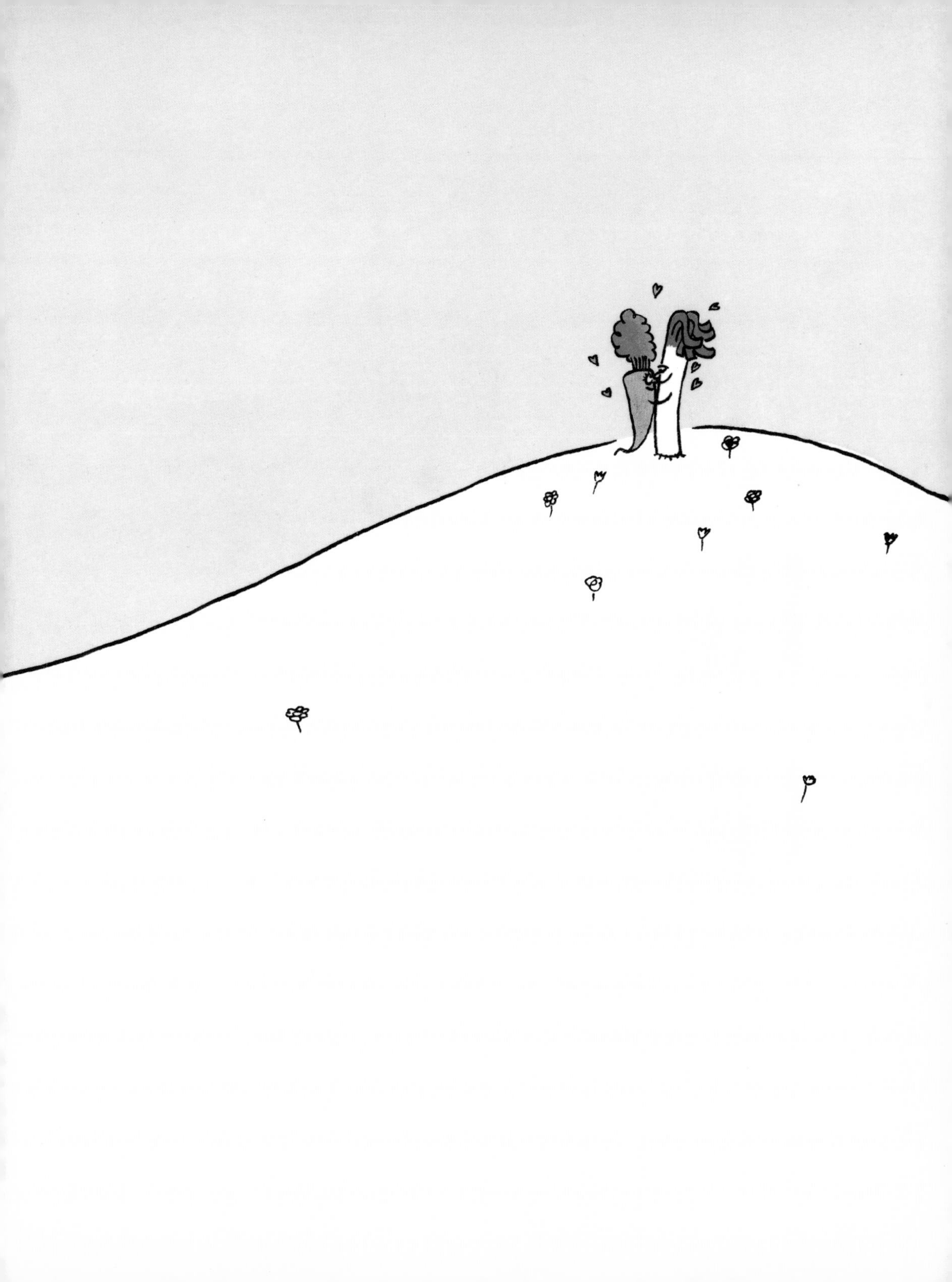

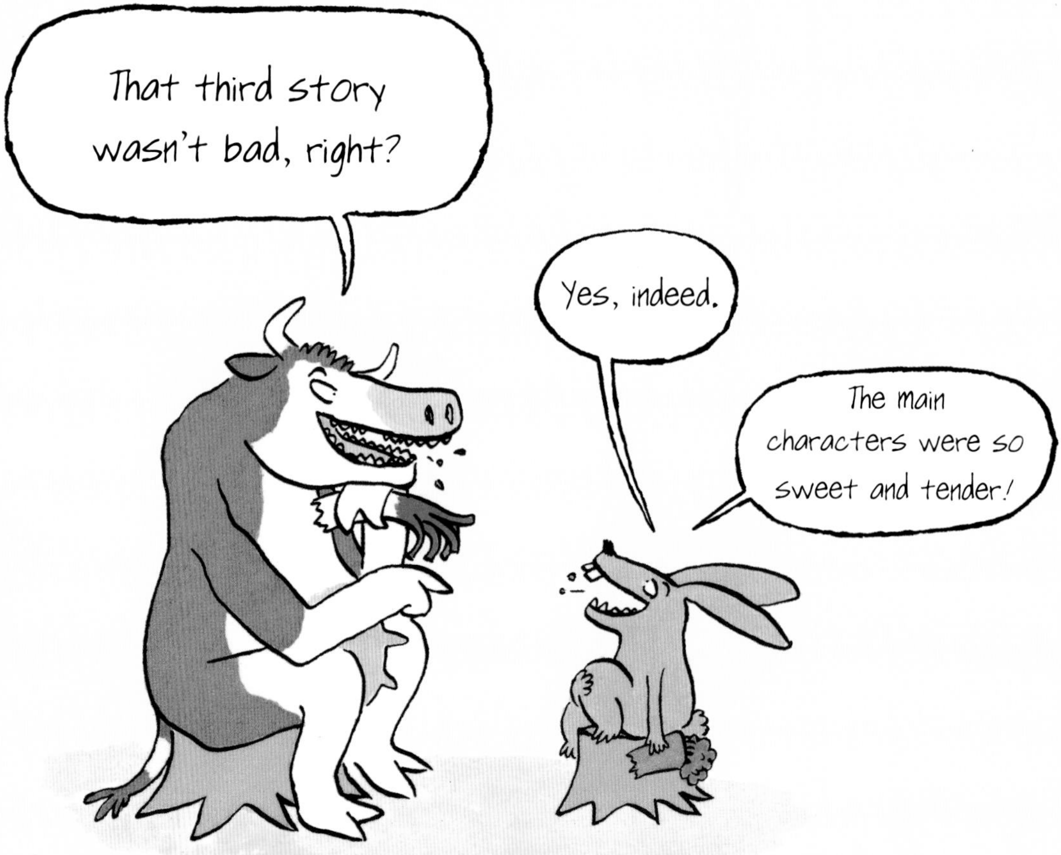
That third story wasn't bad, right?
Yes, indeed.
The main characters were so sweet and tender!